MW00929852

Reminded

Rose of Petrichoria

Book 3

By Katie Hauenstein

For my readers,
I am so glad you have loved this story
as much as I loved writing it.

Table of Contents

Prologue

"Who are you again?" I ask the man who looks like Peter, but isn't Peter. We're in the treehouse that Stephan and I used to sit in."

"David," he says.

"Oh. That's right," I murmur. "And how do I know you?"

"I was your husband in your false life."

Horrified with myself that I forgot – again – I reply, "Right. Sorry."

"There's no need to be sorry, Miriam. Remember, I'm only in your head, so there's no one really to offend."

We sit in silence again as I contemplate what he said. I had thought getting my memories back would fix everything, but now, I feel more lost than ever before, especially since everyone I loved is now dead.

"I don't know who I am anymore," I say to David – to myself. "When I remembered everything and lost my false life, I think I lost a piece of me. Is there a way to get it back?" I look to him in vain. If I don't know the answer to that question, surely he doesn't either.

Sure enough, he shrugs. "I don't know. I suppose only time will tell."

"Where is Harrison?" I ask in an abrupt change of subject. "Why haven't I seen him? Why do I only see you? No offense."

"Remember –"

"I know. I know. I can't offend you. You are me. And you don't know anything more than I do."

Frustrated, I stand and brush the dirt and dried leaves off my rear-end. Without a word to David, I climb down the tree to see if Harrison is somewhere else in my dreamscape.

I run through the familiar woods behind Evergreen Palace, away from the safe haven of my childhood treehouse. As I run, I yell for Harrison. Where is he?

"Harrison! Harrison! I need you!"

When I approach the palace, I go straight to the center of my rose maze. I miss coming here in real life. Right now, it's safe – Frank can't find me in my dreams. Or so I think.

"Miriam!" Frank is calling for me, taunting me. "Come on, love. Come to me!"

Without wanting to, my body obeys. I get off my bench and walk straight to him. My brain screams at my body to stop or run and hide, but it disobeys; it will only listen to Frank.

"There you are," Frank says as he traces a finger along my jaw. "When are you going to learn, Rose? You have nothing and no one left, but me.

I woke up with a start, drenched in sweat and struggling out of the arms of my captor. I hated it when dreams went from in control to out of control so quickly. It seemed to be happening more and more lately.

"Wha – what's going on, Rose?" Frank mumbled. "Your side of the bed is soaking. Are you alright?"

"It's 'Miriam,' Francis" I said sternly. "And I'm fine and dandy, you rotting weed," I mumbled so he couldn't hear me as I strode to the bathroom. Splashing my face with water, I took deep breaths to get over the vividness of the dream portion of my vision. With the stress I was under, the real visions were frequently blending with false dreams. I knew Frank hadn't really been in my mind, but it was still disconcerting.

In my peripheral vision, I saw Frank come in. "Can I help you with something, Francis?" I snapped.

"Are you going to shower or something?"

I looked at him incredulously.

"What?" He asked. "Seriously. I can't hold you when you're like – this." He said "this" with a wide up-and-down gesture referring to my whole body. I knew what he was getting at, I was soaked with my perspiration and stunk to the highest evergreen. Any other time, I definitely would have showered.

With a smirk and fake yawn, I said, "You know, I think I'm too tired to deal with it right now. I'll shower in the morning." With a gentle shove against his chest, I pushed my way past him back towards the bed.

"You have *got* to be yanking my roots." Frank said, exasperated. "You're going to take every chance you can to make my life miserable, aren't you?"

Tucking myself back into the disgustingly wet bed, I simply said, "Yup."

With a groan, Frank climbed in the other side. I felt his hand try to go around my waist, but he shuddered and pulled away. Thank goodness.

Before going back to sleep, I wished that Harrison would make an appearance in my mind. Something told me that he was trying to figure out a way to rescue my kingdom and me, but it would be nice to hear it from him.

Knowing wishing wouldn't get me anywhere, I closed my eyes to go back to sleep. For the first time since his takeover, I was able to sleep the rest of the night without Frank's grubby hands all over me.

Part I

Chapter 1

In all my years at Evergreen Palace, I had never seen the rain flood the fields and forest floor like it had been doing for the last several days. It was as if the sky wept along with me for our great loss. Frank and his, now deceased, father had taken everyone and everything I held dear, and had them killed or destroyed.

Five days had passed since Frank and his people overthrew my parents' rule and killed them. That day, I discovered he and his people were responsible for a lot more death, too. They were responsible for the mutated Daze that killed the Noble families ten years prior, and the explosion that killed Ella and Thomas, too. On my wedding day, they added my parents, King George XV, Queen Domonique, and Peter, along with anyone in the streets who dared to stand against them, to their kill count.

When my memories returned, I celebrated. Even when I realized that I had forgotten my false life, I still celebrated. Surely, I figured, that part of me wasn't all that important. I was wrong. I couldn't remember anything from it anymore. There was the man who visited me in my dreams, but during waking hours, I couldn't remember who he was or why he was important to me.

Without those memories and experiences, I felt like a giant piece of me was missing. I knew that false memories of acting classes helped me through the final part of my first time in Frank's captivity, but those were long gone and useless to me.

Being aware of all the loss and death I had gone through only made matters worse. Not only had I lost Father, Mother, and Peter all in the same day, but with my real memories back, I knew of all those Nobles – and my friends – that I lost to the mutated Daze.

What a failure at life I am. It was Doctor Winston all along. He was right under my nose the whole time! The vials were right in front of my face! How did I miss it? And now? Now I've lost the last of my loved ones and my kingdom to a maniac. Maybe I should just give it over – it's not like I would do a better job. No. Frank can't keep Arboria. I have to figure out a way to get it back. But how? I'm alone in this.

Sighing, I shook my head and stared out the window again, wallowing in self-pity and pessimism. My wallowing only lasted a moment, though, as the sky darkened enough for the red light on the Space Needle to illuminate. At the moment, it was the highlight of my day and it brought a smile to my face. The Space Needle acted as a beacon to the rest of the kingdom of Arboria to indicate how safe things were.

There were only three people who knew where the switch was to change it back to green: the ruler by blood, the heir, and the Arborian Guard who was placed in charge of it. Father was killed and I was not being cooperative in either telling how to switch it back to green or who the Guard with the proper knowledge was. It was Frank's father, so that knowledge would do them no good anyway, but I kept that to myself. Anything to make Frank a little more miserable.

Every night, when the light turned red, it was a small victory for me. No one would wander into Petrichoria thinking all was well. Not that anyone would have thought that. The wedding was holocommed to the world, so everyone knew of Frank's treachery and the betrayal of Prince Phineas of Britainnia – my former betrothed.

Because Frank had the holocomm removed from our room, I had no idea what time it was, but I was figuring it was around 6:00 since it had become dark. Frank usually showed up shortly after dark. Sure enough, a moment after my estimation, the door slid open and King Francis walked in, catching me smiling.

"It's nice to see you smile, Rose," he said, leaning against the doorframe.

Wiping the smile off my face, I said, "It's 'Miriam,' Francis." I felt another small victory when his left eye twitched and jaw clenched at the use of his real name. The reaction was one of the only joys in life I had left. He preferred me to call him Frank – admittedly, I still called him 'Frank' in my head – but I had no desire to do any little thing to make him happy. "The Space Needle turned on. It is the highlight of my day right now."

Frank bristled at the reminder that there was something he couldn't control. Shoving his hands in his pockets, he began to walk over to me. "What will it take for you to call me 'Frank' again?"

"What will it take for you to stop calling me 'Rose?'"

Frank threw his hands up in irritation. "Come on! It has been days, Rose. No one is going to save you from your perceived danger."

Looking at my hands, I said, "It has only been five days, Francis."

"You only have *nine* days left until you have to give yourself to me," he said, just as he had reminded me every night before bed for the last five nights when he cuddled into me.

"Fourteen nights."

"Thirteen nights."

"Twelve nights."

"Eleven nights."

9

"Ten nights."

"I do not need a reminder."

The truth of the matter was that I was not waiting to be saved. I was waiting for the right moment – and the bravery – to run away. Someone out there would harbor me and I would find the people organizing to retake the Crown.

There has *to be someone.*

Though I had not received word from anyone, there was no way for anyone to get a hold of me, I knew they were out there. Enough soldiers from the Royal Arborian Guard had managed to escape from death and they would not give up without a fight.

Frank finished his stroll over to me and bent to his knees. Taking one of my hands in his, he tilted my face up with the other so I had to look at him. "You will be joining me for dinner tonight. The Nobles have returned home to get their provinces under control and I do not wish to eat alone."

"Very well, husband."

He smiled like he had won, but really, I was only agreeing because it was the first opportunity he had given me to leave the room. Being out and about would allow me a chance to see his new security measures.

"I would like for you to get dressed. I am sure you can manage that without Adele?"

"Of course, I can. I can even brush my own hair and apply my own makeup. I am not inept, Francis."

"Frank. I will have a surprise for you in the morning, though."

I shrugged. "If you insist on calling me 'Rose,' I will call you 'Francis.' To get respect from me at any level, you must earn it."

Frank pursed his lips together, then walked over to the closet. I knew he was picking my clothes out. He only let me choose my nightgown the first night of my new captivity, our wedding night. The night we agreed he would wait to take my virginity until Christmas night so I had time to adjust to my new life. Little did he know, I was planning on being gone long before then.

He came out with a navy blue dress lined with buttons in the back that we both knew I would need help with. "Well played, sir," I said, snatching the dress from his hands as he chuckled to himself about how clever he was. After stopping off at the closet myself to get undergarments, I went into the bathroom.

I stripped off my nightgown and underwear and hopped in the shower to clean up. I knew I had let myself go over the last few days and made a mental decision to begin taking care of myself after that night. After toweling off, I stuck my long hair in the dryer and brushed it out. I quickly applied some simple makeup, pulled the dress over my head, and walked out of the bathroom.

Even though I was sure he heard me come in, Frank didn't look at me. He was sitting in the spot I had claimed by the window.

"The rain has been flooding the streets," he said simply as he walked over and began doing my buttons. Since I didn't want to give him the wrong idea, I tried not to shiver in revulsion as his fingers brushed my skin.

Clearing my throat and wiping the grimace he couldn't see from my face, I asked, "Did you order the street cleaners to check the pipes that drain the water to the Petrichorian Sound? They sometimes become clogged with branches and other debris."

He stopped buttoning and stepped in front of me with a confused look on his face. "What?"

"Sometime in January we have the pipes cleaned out. However, if it has been a particularly rainy or stormy season, they require cleaning sooner."

"I didn't know that," Frank said, looking back out the window, then stepping behind me to finish buttoning me up. This time when his knuckles brushed my skin, I couldn't help the shiver. Luckily, he seemed to be too distracted by what I had said to react.

I sighed. "There are probably lots of little things you don't know."

He finished the buttons, stepped in front of me again, and held me by the waist. "Like how to switch the Space Needle from red to green and vice versa and who the Guard responsible for it is?"

I smirked. "Yes. Like that. If you would like to escort me to my office, I will make the proper calls before dinner to get the streets cleared."

Frank furrowed his brow. "You would do that?"

"Why wouldn't I?"

"To spite me?"

"I will not make my people suffer any more than necessary under your rule. Anything I can do to make it easier, I will do."

Frank took both my hands in his and looked at them. "I will be good to them."

I closed my eyes and clenched my teeth. "Just take me to my office, Frank."

"Ah. You called me 'Frank.' All I need to do is get you riled up enough to lose track of your thoughts."

"Whatever."

Chuckling, he offered me his arm and I took it with a repulsed grunt. When we walked out the door, I was disappointed not to see Louis standing guard. Adele had said he refused to leave, which told me he followed through with his vow to falsify fealty to Frank.

Seeing as though he had always served as my day Guard, it was a long shot to think he would be there that evening.

I made eye contact with the new guard and recognized him as the man I had spoken with outside my tent when I was in captivity. He bowed with a sympathetic expression on his face. Perhaps Frank's own people were beginning to see him as the mad man he was. After all, what man locks up his wife in her room for five days straight?

We continued past him and he followed at an appropriate distance. Because people were still awake, the lights were on, though they were dim. On our way down the Core, I recognized several palace employees as those who had been there before Frank. I wondered how many stayed for me and how many had been traitors to begin with. If I managed to retake the Crown, it was going to be a nightmare to figure out.

Finally, we arrived at my office and I immediately went over to my Computer Desk to get the information I needed to contact the street cleaners.

"Stop!" Frank said sternly as I began to sit down.

I did, giving him a questioning look.

"What do you think you're doing?"

"Uh – getting the contact information for the street cleaners," I responded in a way that told him he should have been able to figure that out on his own.

After making his way behind me, so he could watch over my shoulder, he said, "Go ahead."

Shaking my head with frustration, I finished sitting and pulled up the information I needed. When I turned to move to my holostation, Frank didn't move from behind me. "I need to get over to my holostation, Francis." He stepped aside and followed me across the room.

I tried dialing up the street cleaners' business address first and no one answered. Then I tried the Director's home address. His wife answered. "Queen Miriam! Oh, thank God you are alright! We have been so worried in the city."

"I am physically alright. At the moment, Francis has me trying to get a hold of your husband to get the pipes cleared. The streets are flooding."

"Oh. Um – I am afraid that is not going to be possible, Your Majesty." The woman sniffled. "My husband was fiercely loyal to you and was among those killed by the traitors." Tears filled the woman's eyes. "They were all down at the station getting ready to do just what you are asking, so the streets would be perfect for the post-wedding celebration, when the fighting began. All the men and women there were killed because no one would offer fealty to Francis Miller."

I sighed. "I am very sorry for your loss. Your husband's loyalty to my family and me is much appreciated. I only hope there are more like him out there. Do not say anything more, however, because Francis is right behind me."

Though I didn't see it, I felt his grip tighten on the back of my seat, which told me his jaw clenched again. I smiled inwardly.

"Yes, Your Majesty. I am sorry I could not have been more help."

"That is alright. Thank you for the information. You and yours are in my thoughts and prayers."

"Thank you, Your Majesty."

I disconnected the comm and looked at Frank. "Brilliant. Thanks to your stupidity, it looks like we will be taking a trip down to the pipes ourselves."

Chapter 2

Frank looked at me as if I had grown an extra head. "What do you mean *we* will be cleaning the pipes?"

"I *mean* you and your people killed the director and everyone who was present during your rebellion. We do not have the luxury of time to wait until tomorrow to go through the whole system of employees. We will need two other men to go with us."

I brushed past him and began my way back up the Core. He must have still been shocked because it took him a while to catch up. "You and I are going down into the pipes?" With every question, his voice grew hilariously higher in pitch.

"Yes, Francis. And two of your men. Father and I join them every other year for the debris clean out just in case of something like this happening. I used to whine about it because I never foresaw a situation that would require me needing to go down there, but it looks like Father was right. As usual."

"What exactly does it entail? Am I going to be swimming in poop?"

By the time he asked that question, we had hit the top of the Core again and I looked at him like he was an idiot because he was one. "We aren't going through the sewage system, Francis. We are going through the street pipes. Most of what's down there is garbage and tree debris. Now – I'm assuming my wetsuit is in my old room since I didn't see it –"

Frank blocked my path. "You can't go in there. Let me get it."

I pursed my lips and shoved him hard out of my way and he stumbled. "I will go in there if I rotting well please." After a quick rush to the door, I slammed on the button to open it and went right in – finding Phin sitting on *my* sofa.

"You weed!" I screamed at him with my nails bent like claws. The shock of seeing Phin so casually existing in my old room caused me to pause just long enough for Frank to catch up to me and grab me around the waist to prevent my attack. Phin jumped from his seat and ran into the bathroom, closing the door behind him. "Coward!" I screamed at Phin. "Let me go, Frank!"

"Rose, we don't have time for this! You said so yourself!" Frank was trying to reason with me as he pulled me back to the door. Like a child, I swung my arms out and gripped the doorway. "Guards! I need your help here!" Frank shouted.

Tentatively, the guards came forward and pried my fingers from the doorway. Whipping my arms frantically, I fought against them, scratching hard enough to draw blood from at least one of the two guards who came to help Frank. When the three of them got me back into my parents' room, my room now, Frank screamed, "Go! Lock us in here!"

"But – Your Majesty! It is not safe!" One of the guards protested.

"You do not think I can handle my wife? Get out!" Frank responded.

Guard One nodded to Guard Two and they quickly left, locking the door behind them. Frank released me, probably thinking I would be subdued by the lock, but seeing Phin in *my* room had driven me over the edge of my sanity. I turned and clocked him in the jaw,

16

surprising him and sending him straight to the floor. Without hesitation, I jumped on him and continued to punch him, scratching him once with a prayer it would scar.

When he stilled, I stopped, not sure why, but didn't move from my spot of victory atop him. Shaking with anger, I brought my bloody hands – not from my blood – to my face and began to cry. Never had I been a violent person. Never had there ever been a time I couldn't be reasoned with.

However, these two men were directly responsible for the deaths of my parents and the loss of my kingdom. The moment I saw Phin, revenge consumed my mind. I could have easily killed him – killed them both. In fact, I probably *should* have killed Frank the moment he stopped moving, but, as I said, I was no longer sane.

I just sat there, straddling him as he lay unconscious, or so I thought, from my beating. After a I wept for a few moments, Frank sat up and grabbed my wrists gently, pulling them from my face. My hands were still shaking as he pulled me against his chest. I hated him. I hated him more than I hated anyone ever in my whole life.

"Do you feel better now?" he asked.

"No," I responded honestly. "I should have killed you while I had the chance."

He sighed deeply. "I'm glad you didn't."

"I'm not."

He pulled away and grabbed my face in his hands. "I understand you hate me and you hate Phin, but for now, I need you to get a grip for our people. We need to get the streets clear."

"*He* needs to be out of *my* home by the morning. Do you understand?"

"Where will he go?"

"Not my problem."

With him holding my face, I had no choice, but to look at his. Bloodied and bruised from my attack, he still managed to look at me like I was his sun and moon. The mad man made no sense in his crazy love for me. In the moment, though, he was being more reasonable than me. He was right. We needed to clear the streets.

"Fine," he acquiesced.

"Fine. Go get my gear from my room," I said, feeling defeated.

"You have to get off me first. As much as I want this some other time."

"Shut up, Francis," I muttered as I stood up and he chuckled. "I'm going to go wash your blood off my hands."

"You can fight. I'll give you that," he said as he walked to the door.

"Wait!" I said and he stopped to look at me. I muttered, "I need your help with the stupid buttons."

Chuckling again at his small victory, he strolled over and gradually undid each button. "This wasn't quite the way I pictured me undoing these tonight, but duty calls." When he was finished, he left me alone to get my wetsuit and give me time to clean up.

As I shuffled my way to the bathroom, I obsessed over how I lost a golden opportunity to take Frank out. I had him down and out. All I had to do was strangle him or put a pillow over his face or – any other number of simple ways to off him, but I didn't. I stopped. I was weak.

Looking at my reflection, I hardly recognized myself. My face, hands, and clothing were splattered with the blood of probably three men, my makeup had run, and my hair was everywhere.

Who have I become? Who is this woman looking at me in the mirror? I am the Queen of this kingdom and I could not even kill a single man to defend it. I don't deserve the Crown.

Finally, I had my life back and everything had been taken away from me again. What good was having my memories if I had no means of using my knowledge to retake the Crown of Arboria and my life?

I stripped off my bloody clothing and slipped into the shower to rinse off. The water turned pink beneath me as the blood washed off my body and out of my hair. I heard the door of the bathroom slide open and Frank walked in. Quickly, I brought my arms over my important bits to cover up, but he just smirked at me.

"Get out, Frank," I said rather than screamed.

Frank only shrugged and turned to the mirror, turning on the sink and starting to rinse the blood from his face and hands. "I need to clean up, too. Granted, I'm not as messy as you were, but still –"

I gaped at him as he continued to clean up. His eyes met mine in the reflection and he gestured small vertical circles with his hands. "Go ahead. Don't let me stop you."

"I'm done anyway," I said somewhat honestly. I wasn't as clean as I would like to be, but I was clean enough to complete our mission. Shutting off the shower, I turned around and reached back for a towel, fully aware that he was looking at my naked rear. There was nothing to be done. Between the three areas of privacy, I was least concerned about him seeing my bum.

Wrapping the towel around me like a strapless dress, I stepped out of the shower and out of the bathroom. Back still facing the bathroom, where Frank was, I toweled off, then began suiting up in the wetsuit he had set on the bed. "There should be wetsuits down at the station for you to borrow, though you should probably have one made for yourself for situations like this," I said, knowing he was watching me.

"It doesn't bother you that I'm watching you get dressed?" he asked as he made his way slowly over to me.

After I was covered enough, I turned around and finished zipping the suit up over myself. The only thing I needed to put on was my mask, but that could wait until we got there. "Of course it bothers me, but arguing about it won't do any good, and we have more important things to worry about right now – like the safety of our people."

"Our people?"

"It is what it is, for now."

"You really aren't going to give up, are you?"

"Are the hovers and your men ready to go?"

Frank sighed at the subject change. "Yes, they are waiting downstairs, but –"

"Then, let's go." I walked over to the door and banged on it. "Open up. We are ready to go!" No one responded and I shot Frank a dirty look. He repeated the exact same thing I had just said and the door slid open, revealing a very scratched up guard. I smiled demurely at him as I walked past and he bowed respectfully, though I was sure he wasn't really feeling it at the moment.

Frank and I speedily made our way down the Core and out the door. As we climbed into the hover, I prayed my battle with Frank hadn't wasted too much time and that we would be able to clear the streets before the flooding became too bad.

Chapter 3

Because we lived in a very rainy part of the world, our curbs were high and slanted to prevent flooding of the buildings that lined the streets. Unfortunately, the rain had been coming down so hard and fast, the water was beginning to lick the floor of the sidewalks. The lights of most businesses were dark and the homes above were lit with candles to prevent the bugs seeking shelter in the homes of humans.

The drive to the station near the city's edge was not very long, and I hopped out of the hover before it was stopped. Frank and the two men he had selected followed me into the building, where no one had bothered cleaning up the bodies of the men and women who had been killed days earlier. The stench of bodies beginning to decay filled the air and I gagged. When I saw them all, I turned to Frank and said, "You need to fix this problem after we fix the problem of the water. *Your* people killed *these* people and it will be *your* responsibility to make sure the dead, *all* of the dead, get proper burials. Am I understood?"

Frank nodded with a shocked look on his face. Gingerly, we stepped over the bodies and I led the men into the locker room where we would be able to find wetsuits for them. I pointed across the room and told them to suit up and they all went over there.

While I waited outside the locker room, I surveyed the carnage surrounding me. There were easily fifty dead in the warehouse-type building. Fifty dead loyal men and women. In that moment, any doubt I had concerning whether or not I could surrender control to Frank was lost. Knowing there had to be more people like that all over the kingdom, I knew I could not let all these people's deaths be in vain.

When Frank walked out with his men, he nodded curtly to me to let me know he was ready. I placed my mask over my face and gestured for the men to do the same. I held up two fingers to let them know to switch to channel two on their built-in comms so we could communicate.

"Follow me, gentlemen," I said in test and all three men gave me a thumbs up to indicate they heard me. As we made our way to the pipe entrance, we continued to have to step over bodies. At the pool room, where we would enter, I turned and gave quick instructions to not stray far as we strapped on our breathing apparatuses. All we needed to do was gather debris and guide it to the pipe's end that emptied into the Sound. When the pipes were clear, we would use the handles on the side like a ladder to pull our way back to the pool room. If there was too much garbage, we would have a longer night out in the Sound collecting it into bags.

Before anyone else could go in, I stepped down into the pool and swam into the main pipe, letting the three men take the three other tinier entrances. I always hated breathing in the mask because it made me feel claustrophobic; being in the smaller tunnels made it worse.

Surprisingly, my pipe was pretty clear and I wondered if it was the problem after all. Allowing the slowed current to carry me, I guided the couple sticks I saw toward the tunnel's opening. As I got closer to the end, I could clearly see the problem: bloated bodies were blocking the exit. There were any number of street entrances they could have come from.

"Rotting weeds," I heard one of the guards say. He must have seen the same thing I did.

A few moments later, Frank tried speaking. "Miriam, I – "

I interrupted. "I do not want to hear it, Francis. Let us just get this done."

Trying not to weep, I set about doing my job. Turning each body so they would fit through the pipe, I tried to keep a cool head, but it was difficult. There were so many and I began to wish I hadn't picked the city's main pipes. After easily a half hour of clearing bodies, the last one was released to the Sound's deep. I grabbed the handles and pulled my way back against the current, which had returned to its usual, fast speed.

When I resurfaced in the pool room, I saw the other three men with grim expressions waiting for me. Frank looked as if he was going to say something. Pulling my mask from my face, I held up a hand and said, "Don't. Just – don't. Your job tomorrow is to take care of the dead. Make sure your Nobles in each province have all their pipes cleared."

Frank nodded as he and his two guards stood to follow me back into the main part of the station, over the dead bodies, and into the hovers to return to Evergreen Palace. We were silent the whole way. I stared blankly out the window, watching as the water cleared from the streets. Hopefully, businesses would reopen soon.

As we rode in silence, a small figure caught my attention. It was the little girl Phin and I had met when we took our walk in the street.

"Stop the hover," I said loud enough I knew the driver heard. When he didn't obey, I yelled, "Stop the rotting hover!"

Startled, the driver stopped and I jumped out of the vehicle into the rain with Frank yelling after me. I rushed over to the child. "Hello?" I shouted over the rain and she looked at my face. "Do you remember me?"

In shock, she nodded her head. "Princess Miriam," she said in a small voice.

"Queen now, honey," I corrected kindly. "Where is your mama?"

Her lips quivered and eyes blinked quickly in a way that answered my question without her needing to say a word. Her mother was dead. "Daddy?" I asked and her expression grew worse. "Come along." I held out my hand and she took it.

I gently guided her to the grocer I frequented when outside the palace behind us and rang the door chime, knowing that the owner lived in the apartment above. After a few moments, Anna, the elderly woman I knew to be the owner, answered the door and breathed, "Queen Miriam."

"Anna, do you know this little girl?" I asked. The woman looked down at the child and nodded. I asked the girl if she was familiar with the woman and she nodded as well.

"I know things are difficult right now, but because of Francis' ruthlessness, this child has been left without parents. Can I trust you to make sure she is taken care of? I will make sure a stipend is sent to help take care of her and will check in on her often."

"Yes. Of course, Your Majesty. I will do anything I can to help restore order to our kingdom."

"Thank you." I knelt down and took the girl's face in my hands. "What is your name, child?"

"Rose."

I swallowed hard. "Rose, this woman is going to take care of you. I will check in on you in a few days. Be a good girl, alright?"

"Yes, my Queen." She threw her arms around my neck and wept. I let her, allowing her tears and the rain to soak me even more thoroughly than I already was from the pipes. When she was done, the kind woman took her hand and brought her inside.

I stood there for a moment, looking at the closed door and considering the state of Arboria. I had to fix it. When I returned to the hover, Frank didn't chastise me or commend me; he nodded at my order to make sure the family was compensated, then stayed silent the rest of the way to the palace.

At the palace, I dragged myself upstairs and Frank went straight to Father's office, probably to make the comms I ordered him to make. The bloody guard was still standing at the door to my new room. Though he bowed, I didn't bother acknowledging him; he was still bent over when the door slid shut behind me.

The room was lit red from the Space Needle, which matched my mood. I wanted to die. I wanted to end it all and let someone else save Arboria. Perhaps there *was* a resistance and whoever was leading it could become the new ruler. Between the confusion I was feeling at the lack of my false memories and the fact I was blatantly ill-prepared, there was no way I was ready to rule.

Honestly, I didn't feel I much deserved to be Queen at that point. Even if there *were* bombs planted throughout the major cities of Arboria, I had to wonder if I actually succeeded in saving anyone by giving in to Frank. In fact, the whole evening had convinced me that I had given in too easily.

Petrified by my failure as a Queen, I stood still there, just past the doorway. I stared at one of the tree trunks drenched in red light and imagined it was bleeding along with the rest of the kingdom. How long I stood there, I will probably never know, but eventually I staggered to the bathroom to clean up as much as I could.

After starting the hot water and dumping some rose-scented oil into the tub, I stripped out of the wetsuit, letting my hair loose. A tear fell from my eye and my lower lip began to tremble as I put my hair up into a hasty bun.

Sitting in the bath, I pulled my knees to my chest and cried. I cried for the nameless people who were released to the waters. I cried for my parents. I cried for my kingdom. Selfishly, I cried for myself.

Not wanting Frank to find me naked again, I got out before long, after scrubbing myself red, and slipped on a night gown. Partly, I dreaded falling asleep, though I knew I needed it. Since the takeover, I had no more visions of the future. Harrison didn't visit me, despite my begging for his presence. If the premonitions and visions had been coming from God, I felt as though He had deserted not only me, but Arboria.

Never before had I felt more alone than when I was lying in my bed, awaiting my captor and the dark sleep that would soon overtake my senses.

Chapter 4

The next morning, I woke up in bed alone and without visions again for the third night in a row. Relieved to not have Frank's arms around me, I spread my arms and legs in a giant stretch on the bed and sighed. I spent some time staring at the ceiling before I decided to follow through with the promise I had internally made, to begin taking care of myself, the previous evening.

Given the previous night's events, I was plenty tempted to lay in bed all day, but then I reconsidered when I remembered the room full of bodies and the bloated forms blocking the water pipes. Now was not the time to give up; it was the time to fight.

While I was in my closet, selecting a new navy blue halter dress with a brown shrug, I heard the door to the room slide open. Thinking it was Frank, I sighed loudly. "I'm in the closet, pervo! Still in my nightgown!"

Light footsteps made their way to the closet; footsteps too light to be Frank. Furrowing my brow, I turned to the entrance to see a face I hadn't seen a long time.

"Hello, Queen Miriam," said Marie. My assistant from before the freeze who turned out to be a spy.

Marie.

Marie, who I had considered a friend. Marie, who spied on me and reported to the traitors. I didn't want to believe it when the evidence was shown to me.

"You really were with them," I said.

Marie shuffled her feet and scrunched up her face. "Yes, but I swear. I had nothing to do with the deaths of the Nobles."

"You may not have injected them with the syringes, but you are just as much responsible as anyone else, Marie. Have you spent the last ten years in prison trying to excuse yourself? You're lucky Father didn't have you executed, especially after what happened to me."

Marie cleared her throat. "King Francis has assigned me with the job of being your assistant again. Shall I help you with your corset, Miriam?"

"*Queen* Miriam, Marie. And yes. Whatever." I handed her my clothing and she helped me into it. She applied some light makeup and braided my hair in silence before taking her leave.

I sat myself down on the large blue sofa Frank had brought into the room. As I was considering how odd the color was in Evergreen Palace, the door slid open and a disheveled Frank shuffled in. Between the clear exhaustion in his body language, and the bruises and scratches on his face, he was truly a piece of morbid art. I was quite proud of my work.

Quirking a brow, I asked, "Are you just now getting in?"

He looked over to me and matched my quirked brow with one of his own. "Are you awake and ready for the day?"

Crossing one leg over my other, I simply said, "Indeed. *Marie* helped me."

"So you received your surprise?"

"Yes. Thank you for the return of my traitorous assistant," I said with sarcasm.

Sighing, he walked over and dropped himself hard on the sofa next to me. "Long night. Seems as though the major cities were all having similar problems that Petrichoria had. I made orders to make sure any further dead are dealt with immediately, on top of orders to properly take care of the bodies in existence now."

I pursed my lips and tried not to cry about how he casually talked about the dead. "Are there a lot of people dead?"

"Many more than I anticipated," Frank said sadly.

"Do you expect there will be even more?"

"It's hard to tell," he said with a heavy sigh. "People are just so rotting loyal to your family. Many aren't willing to swear loyalty to a new monarch."

"Can't blame them. It's not like there was any problem with the previous monarch."

Frank ignored my comment. "I mean – it's not like I am incorporating a *completely* new monarchy. You're still here. That should legitimize things in the eyes of the people."

"It probably would have if you hadn't killed everyone and forced me to marry you in the most public way possible."

Frank twirled a loose blue string from the arm of the sofa and examined it. "I'm going to shower and change, then we're going down to the Throne Room."

I furrowed my brows. "What Throne Room?"

Standing, he answered, "I disbanded the Arborian Council and had the Council Chamber transformed into a Throne Room."

"You did what?!"

As he made his way to the bathroom, he said dismissively, "I am going to be making a lot of changes. Just get used to it."

The door slid shut behind him with me still gaping at him. Hardly believing what I had just heard, I shook my head a few times to pull myself together. Every time I thought I could handle anything he threw at me, Frank surprised me with something else.

How am I supposed to do this alone?

At the thought, I realized it was finally around the time when the night guard would switch over to the day guard. Still hearing the shower water running, I went over to the door and tapped on it from the inside.

"Louis, are you out there?" I asked quietly. No one answered.

Perhaps he can't verbally respond.

"Louis, if you are out there, tap on the door once."

Tap.

Thank God!

"I am so glad you are here. Thank you for your loyalty."

Tap.

With a feeling of great relief, I walked back over and sat on the sofa just as the shower shut off. Frank walked out of the bathroom in a towel a couple of minutes later and I shut my eyes. He chuckled and said he was going into the closet to get dressed.

Not trusting that comment, I kept my eyes shut until he walked over and stroked my cheek with his hand. I jolted back and he chuckled again – I hated his stupid chuckle. When I opened my eyes, I gave him a death glare. Remembering he was insane helped me understand how he could transition from being sad about how many people he was responsible for dying to being a selfish jerk.

Offering me his arm, he said, "Let's go." I stood and took his arm. "You will be happy to know that Louis vowed loyalty to our new monarchy, so he is still serving as your day guard."

I gave a false sigh and shake of my head. "While I am glad he is alive and still here, it is disappointing he swore fealty to you. At least there is one proper Arborian Guard left at the palace."

We walked out and I gave Louis a sad look to go along with the part I was playing and he dutifully kept a neutral expression on his face. Noticing the interaction, Frank said into my ear, "While I would like to think Louis swore fealty to *me*, I am sure he only stayed to look after you. I have no problem with that. I know you are safe with him."

I simply nodded and allowed him to escort me down the Core, the rest of the way to the new Throne Room. When I saw the intricately carved cherry wood thrones, I stopped in my tracks. Frank had clearly had them commissioned long ago; the work was intricate. One had patterns of thorns and sharp leaves and the other had a beautiful floral pattern. Because my family, and our ancestors, had always striven for some form of equality in our governing, we never had thrones, or a Throne Room, for that matter.

"What do you think, Rose?"

"Miriam," I muttered.

Frank chuckled as he took his seat on the masculine throne and I shuffled my way up to the other one. "Do you seriously expect for me to sit in this every day?" I asked.

"This is the way we will do things now," Frank said. "In fact, I believe we have a prisoner due here any moment."

Not fully registering what he said, I sat down on the plush blue cushion set into the throne carved for me. Before the experience could soak in, the door to the room slid open and a man dressed in the uniform of the Royal Arborian Guard was thrown to his knees before us. It was then I recognized him.

"Earl!" I jumped to my feet only to be shoved down by Frank, who sauntered forward. My heart raced, hoping in vain that nothing terrible was about to happen. Earl's apologetic gaze met mine and I shook my head slightly as if to tell him there was nothing to be sorry for.

"Earl, Earl, Earl," Frank taunted as he circled Earl with his hands folded behind his back. Louis shuffled nervously at the back of the room. "I am so much more than a participant in the King's Test now, am I not? Tell me," he lowered himself to a squat so he was at eye level with Earl, "What am I now, Earl?"

Without missing a beat, Earl said, "A traitor." His comment earned him a backhand to the face and he stumbled to the floor. Blood was seeping through slices in his back, which made me wonder what kind of torture poor Earl had already endured.

"I am your King!" Frank yelled like the mad man he was. "And you would do well to remember that!"

"I am loyal only to Queen Miriam," Earl said breathlessly. Frank looked at me in a way that said he wanted me to correct him, but I only folded my arms across my chest and tilted my chin up.

In a menacingly quiet voice, Frank said, "Queen Miriam is *mine* now. There is nothing you or your pathetic band of loyalists can do about it."

Band of loyalists?

"We will not give her up without a fight," Earl said.

We?

"Tell you what, Earl. I want to make a deal with you." With a gesture from Frank, the door slid open again and a middle-aged woman was dragged to the opposite side of the room from Earl. Earl closed his eyes and pressed his lips tightly together.

"Don't tell him anything, Earl!" the woman shouted and the guard behind her placed a heavy hand on her shoulder.

"Her name is Emma, right? Earl and Emma. Sounds sweet. How long have you been married?" Frank spoke in a deceptively gentle voice.

Married? This is Earl's wife!

"Frank –" I said cautiously and he held a finger up to silence me.

"Answer the rotting question!" Frank screamed with spittle flying all over Earl's face.

"Twenty-five years, Frank," Earl responded with wet eyes.

"Twenty-five years," Frank repeated calmly, ignoring Earl's lack of formality. "How much do you love your silver wife, Emma?"

"More than life itself," Earl sobbed. Since his hands were cuffed behind his back with mangacuffs, he was unable to set himself up after Frank backhanded him. It was so sad to see him curled on the floor like that.

"Please, Frank. Do not do this," I said, slowly rising from my seat.

With fury, Frank jumped up and spun around, facing me. "Sit in your seat of office, Miriam!" he yelled at me. I did, not knowing why I was obeying him. Emma wept along with her husband.

Frank turned and lowered himself again. "This is the deal, Earl. You tell me where your people are hiding and I will let your wife live. She will be banished, but she will live."

There are people hiding? Organizing?

33

"No! Don't tell him, Earl!" Emma shouted and the guard pointed his weapon to her head.

He wouldn't really do it, would he?

Earl still had his eyes closed, not like he was considering actually giving Frank the information he wanted, but as if he was delaying the inevitable.

"If you tell me, I will let you both live, but I will still have to banish you from Milleria," Frank said quietly.

Milleria? He renamed the kingdom? It sounds like the name of some kind of infectious disease. It is. An infectious disease that has made Arboria ill.

Opening his eyes, Earl mumbled something inaudible. Frank bent closer to hear and Earl spat in his face. "I will tell you nothing," Earl said loudly enough for me to hear.

Frank's eyes bugged out of his head and a vein began pulsing in his neck. I had never seen him so angry. "Fine! Kill her!" Frank yelled.

"No!" I yelled and jumped out of the throne, but as I began to run forward, Frank shot up his hand and I stopped moving involuntarily. He nodded to the guard, who fired the weapon into Emma's head, killing her instantaneously. My brain screamed at my arms and legs to move, but nothing happened. I was completely frozen.

Keeping his hand up, Frank dropped his head and stood upright, walking over to me. "Now, do you see what you made me do, Miriam? You made me show my hand." As he pointed down and spun his hand, I turned and returned to my seat.

Sure my face mirrored Earl's look of horror, I asked, "How are you doing this?"

"I do not know. I discovered I could control people a couple years back. I much prefer *convincing* people to do what I want, which is why I do not do it often. It worked to get my father out of the way, though. And to stop your vicious attack on me last night."

"It really *was* you that killed my parents. I killed an innocent man," I said in mortified realization.

"Yes, you did. Well, innocent in that, at least. Innocent blood on the *good* Queen's hands. Though, I do not know how much I forced him. He wanted to do it – to finish what he started all those years ago – I just helped him out a bit," Frank taunted me.

"But, if you can control me, why haven't you just forced me to allow you to –" I bit my lip, not wanting to complete my question in front of everyone.

Frank leaned over and traced his finger along my jaw. "Like I said, I prefer to convince people to do what I want. Verbal manipulation is so much more satisfying than physical manipulation. Do not think I am beyond it, though."

"Get your traitor hands off her!" Earl shouted from the floor, successfully distracting Frank from me.

"Right," he said softly, still looking me in the eyes. Turning back to Earl, he said, "Final chance, Earl. Tell me what I want to know."

"Never," Earl said simply.

"Very well," Frank said as he marched over to the guard who had just killed Emma. Taking his weapon, Frank turned around and shot Earl several times in the head. With a deep sigh, he said to the guard, "Get these bodies out of here and send someone in to clean this mess." The guard nodded and pointed to Louis to help him.

"You just – you – you –" I looked at Frank.

"I killed him. Yes. I hated him anyway. I am kind of glad he didn't talk."

"Why – why – why didn't –" I was at a loss for words. I was trying to process all the information that had just come my way. Frank renamed Arboria. Frank could *control* people.

"Why didn't I make him tell me what I wanted to know? It doesn't work that way. Not sure why. Maybe I just need more practice," he muttered. Then he shouted, "Bring in the next one!" For the rest of the day, several more people were brought forward and tortured similarly to poor Earl. No one would tell him what he wanted to know. While I was glad he was getting nowhere in his search for the loyalists, the killing was too much for me.

At around 5:00, Frank sighed and rubbed his temples. "No more today, gentlemen." He waved his hand and the guards left the room.

Gentlemen. Pah! They're monsters just like him.

Turning to face me, and taking my hand, Frank said with concern, "Rose, you're looking kind of pale. Should we eat dinner?"

"Are you serious?"

"Yes. You look like you might pass out."

"I just might after what I have seen today."

"I *am* sorry I had to control you. I never wanted to do that. I don't intend to again, unless you try to interfere with my interrogations. Then, I will have no choice."

"That's what you think I find disturbing?" I asked with a cold laugh. That was only a portion of what I was mortified about.

"Oh. You mean Earl."

"And Emma. And Thomas. And Justin. And Zed. And –"

"I get it. I get it. You don't like the killing. I can't blame you." Frank sighed loudly. "If they would only tell me what I want to know, they could live. Really, they're bringing it on themselves."

"Tell you? So – what? So you can go and kill *all* of them? When does it stop, Frank? Just this morning you were morose over all the deaths that have happened because of you. Then, you spend all day adding to the number!"

Pretending like he didn't hear me, he frowned at the hand he was holding and said, "Your hand is so cold."

"You haven't released your hold on my torso, legs, and arms. I haven't moved in hours."

"Roots!" he said and released me. My muscles relaxed and I slumped in my seat. Taking my hand back from him, I rubbed both hands together to try to get my feeling back. "I'm so sorry, Rose. I have been so preoccupied, I forgot."

Preoccupied with torturing and killing people faithful to me.

"Yes. Whatever." I stood and began to go out the door.

"Where are you going?"

I stopped on my own volition and said, "I need to wash the death off me. I'm going to take a shower."

"No. We both need to go to the Dining Hall for dinner. I have special guests coming tonight," Frank said as he joined me and took my hand again, refusing to let me take it back.

"I would really rather not eat tonight."

"You can eat on your own or I can make you eat. It's up to you. Now that you know my secret, there really isn't a reason for me to hold back."

Chapter 5

Preferring not to be played with like a puppet, I allowed Frank to lead me to the Dining Hall. Who our special guests were, I had no idea. It could have been any of Frank's stooges. I only hoped whomever it was did not include Robert Casey – sorry, *Duke* Robert of Maple.

To say I was shocked at who our guests were would be an understatement. When we entered the Dining Hall, Frank separated from me to go shake hands with them and I stood stupefied in the doorway. They all bowed deeply.

"None of that now, Lucas. We are friends, yes?" Frank said as he approached Lucas Flowers.

"Of course," Lucas said with a wide smile as he rose.

"Miriam, you remem –" Frank said, turning as if I was standing next to him, and stopping when he realized I wasn't. Frank waved me over, "Come now, Miriam. Come say hello to our friend, Lucas." Frank gestured with his hand again and I came over, not wishing to be forced.

"Lucas," I mumbled, offering my hand with a furrowed brow. After thinking about Lucas' allegiance to Frank, it made some sense. After all, he *was* from the Willow province, which had been central to Frank's operations before taking over.

"Your Majesty," Lucas said with a smirk and a kiss to the hand. He proceeded to introduce the other people at the table, his bandmates. However, I was too flummoxed to really pay attention to anyone's names. I was able to pull myself together enough to offer my hand to each male member and a nod to the female drummer; I only remembered she was the drummer because those who played the complicated instrument always impressed me.

Uncomfortably, I took my new seat, Mother's old seat, and Frank took Father's old seat. Regardless of the fact the chair was one-of-a-kind, I decided then, I would be burning it and anything else Frank made his own when I retook the kingdom. It was the first time since my disastrous wedding day we sat at the table and it felt weird, to say the least.

Conversation and laughter swirled around me as dinner was served. True to my word, I did not touch my food. Images of Frank brutally killing people all day were seared into my brain, and I was not sure I would recover from it any time soon. How much he seemed to enjoy himself as he shot people in the head and slit people's throats all day caused the fact that he was *generally* so gentle with me to baffle my mind.

As everyone else continued to eat and talk, I sipped at my wine and eyed the instruments on the makeshift stage before me. The setup was typical with a guitar, bass, piano, violin, and drums. A couple microphones were set up, as well. When the thought of dancing crossed my mind, I prayed silently I would not have to.

"Is that not right, dear?" Frank was asking me after the table had been cleared of food and dishes.

"Hmm? Sorry I did not hear you. What was that?" I asked.

Frank frowned at my obliviousness, then rephrased his question. "I was saying we would love to hear Lucas' band play."

"I suppose so," I responded blandly. "The instruments *are* already set up after all."

"Anything for my Queen," Lucas said with glee. It was almost as if he was completely unaware that I was unhappy at his alliance with Frank. He and his bandmates made their way to their instruments and Frank stood up, offering me his hand.

Well, darn. Looks like I will *be dancing with him.*

With a dark look, I took his hand and he led me to an empty space in the Dining Hall. Creepily, he pulled me close and sniffed my hair. "Eight days, my lovely," he whispered in my ear, which sent a chill up my spine.

The band began to play a slow song and Frank's groping went to a new extreme. In my whole life, I had never had a dance partner hold me by the bum rather than my back. Leo had come close all those years ago, but even he never went that far.

"I was thinking of hiring Lucas and his band, Rose," Frank said.

"Is that so, *Francis*?" I asked, emphasizing his name and enjoying the anticipated reaction.

"Frank. It has always seemed odd to me that there is rarely live music in a palace with someone who loves it so much."

Not wanting to display that I actually agreed with him on something, I shrugged. "I suppose it could be nice."

"Perhaps you and Lucas could collaborate and write something for the Christmas Ball?"

That got my attention. "The Christmas Ball?"

"Yes. The ball that happens every Christmas."

"I know what the Christmas Ball is. Do you seriously still plan on having one with everything else that needs to be done?"

"Of course. I figure it will give you something to do while the Millerian Nobles and I get everything up and going again."

Blech. "Millerian" must mean one who is infected with Milleria.

"You do realize that *weeks* of planning usually go into the Christmas Ball and you're giving me a little over one week, right?"

Frank shrugged. "I'm sure your mother was planning it, then. I'll bet she has everything all set up in her office somewhere. Louis can escort you and your assistant there tomorrow."

It bothered me that he referred to Mother so nonchalantly, as if she was gone on vacation and wasn't killed only a few short days ago by his hand.

"Assuming your men didn't kill the florists and caterers," I said sardonically.

The song ended and Frank applauded. I did not. "Very good gentlemen – and lady. You are dismissed for the night. We will discuss a more permanent contract in the morning," Frank said.

"Yes, Your Majesty. It is, and always will be, an honor to serve," Lucas said as he and his bandmates bowed and left.

When they were gone, I sighed. "Can we go to our room now? It's been a long day."

"Yes, my love." Frank took my hand and pulled me up the stairs. When we entered our room, I yanked my hand from his and went into the bathroom. Just wanting to sleep, I took a quick shower and walked out.

"That was fast," Frank said as he brushed past me in my towel.

"I just want today to be over," I muttered.

When he was in the bathroom, I changed into the nightgown he laid out and snuggled into the blue blankets. Now knowing he changed the name of the kingdom, all the blue made sense. He probably changed the colors as well.

42

After a short time, Frank emerged from the bathroom and I sat up. By that point, I was used to the sight of Frank in his boxers. He shook out his short, black hair with his fingers and walked over to me. How could one man, not even a tall man, contain so much evil?

When he laid on his side next to me, I mimicked his position, facing him, and we stared at each other for a few minutes. Finally, I broke the silence.

"Have I ever told you about Stephan?" I asked.

"I don't think so. Was he from your real life or false life?"

"I don't really remember my false life anymore," I responded numbly.

"I'm sorry."

Another long pause sat between us for a bit. "He was like a brother to me. We met when I was two and he was six. He was one of the participants in my first King's Test." I swallowed. "Do you know how he died?"

"I would guess from the mutated Daze my father organized with Doctor Winston."

I laughed dryly. "No. He died from a heart attack during a delusional episode brought on by the mutated Daze. I'm not sure what he was seeing because I wasn't in his head, but I was there. He spent an hour screaming at whatever he was seeing to leave me alone. He was trying to protect me.

"I also sat at the deathbeds of Count Leonard and Count Lincoln. They died covered in boils and rashes with delusions. Linc was experiencing some delusion involving me and tulips, so I told myself I would plant tulips in my garden to remember the seven noblemen that could have become my husband."

Frank frowned. "There are no tulips in your garden."

"No, there aren't. Do you know why?" He shook his head. "I got sick with the Daze before I could. Then, when I woke up, I forgot them. I forgot those men who died so cruelly. Then, when I remembered them, my parents and final friend were brutally murdered, and my kingdom taken from me. I haven't had the opportunity to do it yet."

Frank swallowed hard. "Why are you telling me this?"

"Because, Francis, all those people have died, plus the nameless ones all over the kingdom, so that you could have the opportunity to be King – and you're blowing it. You will not be remembered as a great King, but as a horrid tyrant and I will not truly rest until I have retaken Arboria from you."

With that, I turned over and closed my eyes. After a few moments, Frank pulled me close and wrapped an arm around me like he always did. "Then I suppose you will never truly rest again."

Chapter 6

When I awoke the next morning, Marie was sitting on the sofa waiting for me and Frank was already gone. Sitting up and rubbing my eyes, I asked, "What do you want, Marie?"

"I am here to help you get ready again and plan the Christmas Ball. I hope you do not mind, I took the initiative to go to your mother's office and locate her plans." She held out a stack of papers.

"You went through my mother's things?" I asked with tears building in my eyes and anger causing my voice to tremble. "*I* have not even been allowed out of here to do that. What makes you think you have the right to go through her belongings?"

"I – I did not mean – I did not think – "

"No. You did not!" I shouted and yanked the papers out of her hands. Flipping through them, I traced my fingers over Mother's handwriting and delicate drawings of trees and bells and ribbons. In one, she had designed outfits for Phin and me. I shook my head. Mother loved Christmas. "You did not think," I said more calmly. "Please do not touch anything that belonged to my parents without first discussing it with me again. Understood?"

"Yes, Your Majesty."

"It looks as though everything is planned. Please comm around and make sure the venders are still alive and/or willing to participate. If not, then we will have to do some interviewing."

"Yes, Your Majesty."

"Let us see what you have selected for today." I stood up and followed her to the center of the room, where she helped me into a red halter dress with a brown shrug.

As she applied my makeup, she said, "I wish things were different between us, Queen Miriam. I wish you could see that I meant you no harm before and I mean you no harm now."

"It does not matter what you meant or mean, Marie. The results are still the same."

She nodded and finished up. "I will make these comms, Your Majesty."

"Thank you, Marie," I said as I opened my door and strode out to the Core. Frank must have figured that as long as there was a guard with me, there was no need to keep the door locked. What would I do against a guard? I was surprised to see Louis by himself, though.

Louis followed at his normal distance, and his presence was a balm on my chapped life. I knew he had to be just as horrified as I was on the previous day's happenings, and he had to actually help take bodies away and clean up between prisoners.

"How is your family, Louis?" I asked.

"Safe, my Queen."

"Good." I paused before the Throne Room when I heard male screaming coming from inside. I closed my eyes and braced myself to go in, but couldn't get my feet to make the movement. Could I go in there and endure another day of torture and death? Could I continue do that day after day?

Glancing around, I noticed the hallway was conspicuously lacking in guards. Tossing a knowing look at Louis, I turned away from the door and made my way toward my rose maze instead. When we got to the entrance, Louis tried stopping, but I grabbed his hand and pulled him inside with me instead.

Peering behind us one more time to make sure we weren't being followed, I whispered, "There's a secret exit in my garden that no one knows about. Now's our chance to escape."

Louis' eyes widened. "Are you sure, Your Majesty?"

"Don't question it. There are no guards out there right now for some reason. Now is the time to make our move. I cannot endure this any longer. I will find someone to help me find the loyalists. We have to go."

Louis shook his head. "You go. I will stand guard, so people think you are simply visiting your garden."

"I won't leave without you! You have a family to get to."

"With all due respect, Your Majesty, you must go. Now." Not willing to hear me any longer, Louis turned around and left me alone in the garden.

Should I leave without him? Can I make it anywhere on my own? I have to try.

Swiftly, I ran to the center of the maze and located the hidden floor hatch that led to my secret tunnel. No one knew about this tunnel. Not my parents. Not my Guards. Only the builder and I knew of it, and I hadn't seen the builder in years.

Dust kicked up as I ran down the long tunnel that would let out in the middle of my forest. Coughing and sneezing the whole way, I prayed that the absence of the guards inside didn't indicate that they were checking the perimeter instead.

When I escaped into the crisp, cold winter air, I didn't stop. I was exhausted emotionally and physically, but I knew I had to keep running in order to make it out. Finally, I saw the gate that surrounded the palace grounds and I laughed in relief.

I'm going to make it!

I made a running leap at the gate and climbed it deftly, thanking God that Mother had forced those gymnastics lessons on me. As I swung my legs over the top, my dress caught on the top and caused me to stumble down the other side. I stifled a moan of pain as my ankles clicked with my landing.

Can't stop now.

Limp-running now, I tried to put as much space as possible between the palace and me. Just when I thought I was home-free, I heard a voice, "Your Majesty?"

I stopped in my tracks at the unfamiliar female voice and turned toward it to see four guards in Frank's new blue and brown looking at me questioningly.

"Uh – Hello," I said.

"What are you doing out here, Your Majesty?" she asked.

"Oh – um – you know – getting air."

"A quarter mile from the palace gates?" another guard asked.

"Yes. Well – "

"I think maybe you should come with us back to the palace, Your Majesty," the largest guard said.

"Hmm. I think we will have to agree," I said slowly, "to disagree," I added quickly as I turned to run away. I didn't make it far. The large guard was deceptively fast and caught me before the others even came close.

"Let me go!" I yelled.

"I am sorry, Your Majesty. But you must return. King Francis would literally kill us if we let you go," the female guard said as the brute tossed me over his shoulder and started making his way back to the palace gates.

"You cannot possibly think this is alright!"

"It is what it is, Your Majesty. The sooner you accept King Francis and the new way of things, the sooner things will begin to improve for you," she responded.

"Never!" I shouted and pounded the back of the guard who was carrying me. I got a satisfying grunt of surprise, so I kept doing it, even though he didn't respond again after that.

When we made it back inside Evergreen Palace, Louis came over, frowning. "Put her down immediately! That is your Queen, soldier!" he ordered, and the brute did.

"We found our *Queen* trying to escape outside the palace gates. Aren't you supposed to be watching her?" the brute, with the probably bruising back, asked.

"Your *Queen* is standing right here," I snapped. I waved a pointed finger at all five of them. "When I retake my kingdom and Frank is behind bars awaiting trial for treason, you will all suffer his same consequences. Mark my words."

The brute smirked. "Of course we will, Your Majesty. We gladly serve *King Francis*." With that, the four perimeter guards turned synchronously and left the palace.

"It was worth a try," I huffed. Louis, bless him, acted his part and made no response, not even facially. Soundly defeated, I made my way back to the Throne Room. The little amount of time I spent as a potato sack relieved some of the pain that was in my ankles, so I was able to get around fine. When I got to the doors, I could hear that the screaming was now the higher pitch of a woman. I swallowed and put my shoulders back as I made my way in.

"Ah, Miriam. Late start?" Frank greeted me with blood splattered across his face. I recognized the woman he was torturing as the old Stewardess of our household.

"Francis, please let this woman go," I said.

"No can do, my love," Frank sniffed and wiped the sweat and blood, not his blood, from his forehead. Not even seeming to consider any other option, he gestured with his hands in a manner that controlled my legs to my throne and he sat me down. "I know for a *fact* this woman knows something."

I found that difficult to believe considering the woman's age. She was old enough to be my great-grandmother. "I do not think she knows anything," I responded.

"Shut it!" Frank screamed at me.

"You must not disrespect the Queen," the old woman said, clearly nearing her end.

Frank bent over and said quietly, "You shut it, too, old woman, unless you are going to tell me what I want to know. I *know* he is here. Where is he?"

"Where is who?" I said, perking up.

"No one," Frank said at the same time the old woman said, "Prince Harrison."

Perhaps the old woman did *know something.*

"Harrison is here?" I breathed, hardly daring to believe it.

"No," Frank said at the same time the old woman said, "Yes. Do not give up hope."

Those were her last words. Frank became so infuriated, he slashed her throat. "Gah! Are you happy now? Now I can't get my information from her!" he screamed at me.

"You only have your own temper to blame," I retorted, sickened at the sight of yet another death. "Besides, she was not going to tell you anything."

"No, she wasn't," he said almost to himself as he joined me on his throne. "Clean this up and bring me a wet cloth to clean my face," Frank ordered and guards scattered to listen to him.

"How would you propose I get my answers?" he asked me.

I laughed both from shock that he was actually asking for my advice, and that he actually thought I would give him that advice. "I am not helping you with that, Francis. Seems like that would be more your area anyway."

Frank harrumphed and I smirked despite the gory scene getting cleaned before me. "Phin is gone now, right?" I asked.

With a sidelong glance, he said, "Yes. He has been placed in a safe house in the Willow Province."

"I would rather the loyalists find him and kill him."

"Ha! You had the chance to kill *me* and didn't."

"No. If you remember correctly, you stopped me."

"How would you know I used my ability then?"

"After being under your control for several hours yesterday, I am quite familiar with the feeling. It is horrible; like being trapped in your own body. I would not recommend the experience."

"Duly noted."

When the mess of Frank and the room was cleaned up, we sat there in uncomfortable silence.

"So. How is the Christmas Ball coming along?" Frank asked, attempting small talk.

"Your crony went through my mother's office without me."

"My what?" Frank asked with a tinge of humor.

"Your crony. Marie. She went through my mother's things without asking."

He shrugged. "I'm sure she meant nothing by it."

"Well, it ticked me off."

Frank chuckled. "Did you punish her?"

"No. I just told her not to do it again."

"You didn't punish her?" he asked with incredulous surprise.

"No. There was no reason to. Like you said, she meant nothing by it. I cannot expect you and your heartless minions to understand the emotions that go along with going through one's dead parents' things. Especially *you*."

Frank pursed his lips. "I understand. I cared very deeply for my mother. And my father was my role model."

"So will you raise your spawn to kill you someday? If that is the case, it may be worth giving myself to you in seven days."

"Ha! Well played, Rose."

The rest of the day was spent with mindless banter and random Nobles and Delegates approaching our thrones. Each one attempted to get on my good side, but I was always able to get to them with one snarky remark or another. They should have known better than to think getting on my good side would even be a possibility for them.

By the time dinner rolled around, I was quite pleased with my performance on the throne. I still hated it. Both thrones were on my mental list of palace items to be burned at the end of everything.

Imagine my surprise when Robert Casey was waiting for us in the Dining Hall. I eyed Lucas, who looked apologetic, as if it was somehow his fault Robert was there.

"My Queen," Robert said as he took and kissed my hand, though I certainly didn't offer it to him.

"How much did Francis pay you to let him punch you? Or did you do it for free like a good little henchman?"

Robert blanched. "Rose!" Frank chastised.

I smirked. "Really. I have been curious since finding out you have joined the traitors, Robert. Honestly, the only reason you were sent home after the first round was because you were pervvy and self-absorbed. Had I known you were a traitor, much more drastic measures would have been taken."

Behind us, I heard Lucas choke on a laugh in the microphone. We all turned to look at him and he made some hand gesture for the band to start a new number. When they began playing again, I tilted my head at Robert as if I expected an answer. Frank pinched the bridge of his nose like he couldn't believe me.

"Miriam, really?" Frank asked.

"Yes, really."

"Uh – well – Your Majesty –" Robert stuttered.

"You do not need to answer that question, Robert," Frank said.

"You should if you do not want me to think of you as less of a man than I already do. Listen to me, Robert Casey – sorry – Robert of Maple. My Uncle Edmond, then my cousin Elleouise and dear friend, Peter, belonged to the great Maple Province. I would have had high expectations of anyone who inherited their Province, but you will have higher expectations. Should the people of the Maple Province receive anything less than perfection from you, there will be consequences. Am I understood?"

"Uh –"

So eloquent.

"Did you receive payment for allowing Francis to punch you?"

Robert cleared his throat. "No, my Queen. I allowed it for the good of the movement."

I glared at Robert with a stiff jaw for an uncomfortable moment just to watch him sweat. "Good. I may hate Francis and his minions, but at least you are loyal to someone. May that extend to the people of Maple, however short your tenure may be." Without another word, I made my way to Mother's seat and sat at the table to await the first course.

Watching Francis and Robert exchange pleasantries, it became clear that they did, indeed know each other. Robert was the first of Francis' followers that did not bow or grovel before him. I shifted my focus to the smooth sound of Lucas' voice, the lyrics were something about the stars watching over me and it calmed my soul. It really was strange how Lucas was able to do that when I could hardly stand to look at the man.

"– my Queen?" Robert was sitting next to me and asking me some question. I glared at him, even though I had no idea what he said.

Frank must have noticed my far-away face and said, "Robert was asking what you think of the new color scheme, Rose."

"Color scheme? I did not know you were interested in interior design, Robert. I would not have pegged you for it."

Frank choked on his clam chowder and I patted his back without shifting my gaze from Robert, who only grinned at me. "No, Your

Majesty. I am not into interior design. I designed the new flag for Milleria."

"Milleria," I repeated and sipped at my soup. "I can see where Francis came up with it, obviously, but do you not think it sounds like a disease? A communicable one?"

Frank began choking again, but I did not touch him that time.

"Many countries and kingdoms are named for their founders," Robert pointed out.

"True, but if the name does not flow, it probably should not be used. Look at my ancestor for example, Alexander Nicholls. Nichollsia. Nichollia. No. Just does not work."

"Arboria's founding was much different than Milleria's."

"True. Arboria was not founded by traitors. I digress. I very much like the blues, browns, and ivories." I smiled at him and he grinned back. Frank finally stopped choking and I turned to him. "Everything alright, darling?"

"Everything is wonderful, my love," he croaked.

"This flower has thorns, Frank. Better be careful," Robert chuckled.

"I am aware," Frank responded. "Perhaps she needs a little reminder of what I am capable of."

Robert's easy grin faltered. "What do you mean, Frank?" He gave me a sidelong glance with surprising concern in his eyes. "You will not hurt her will you?"

I blanched and set my spoon down. "He would not dare," I said with uncertainty.

"Of course not, my love. But I *can* make you do other things."

My eyes widened as I looked at Frank and I noticed Robert wiggle uncomfortably in his seat. "I think you perhaps owe Duke Robert a dance," Frank said.

"*I* think I am the Queen and owe no one who follows you the air they breathe," I responded. Then I felt it; his control. I tried to fight it, but couldn't. Like a robot, I stood and turned to Robert and curtseyed in a most unnatural way.

"Frank – I – maybe you should let her go," Robert said, clearly uncomfortable with the turn of events.

"Go ahead, Robert. Dance with your Queen. Just do not try anything."

Clearing his throat, Robert stood and took my hand to lead me to the makeshift dancefloor Frank had arranged when he hired Lucas. Most professionally, Robert placed one hand at the small of my back and held my other.

"You can release me now, Francis. I will dance on my own," I said.

"Call me 'Frank' and I will stop." Frank made me hold Robert even closer and my right eye teared a bit from embarrassment. Robert couldn't meet my forced gaze.

"Frank," I whispered.

"What was that, my love? I cannot hear you from over here." Again, I was pushed closer to Robert.

"Don't give the weed what he wants, Miriam. Just play along," Robert whispered into my ear. I could not look at him because Frank was forcing my cheek against his chest.

"Weed out!" I shouted at him as Lucas began a new song. Frank did not have rhythm as good as mine, but it was good enough to follow Robert. I was surprised at how respectful Robert was, given the situation. Not once during the dance did he cop a feel or say anything rude. Finally, the song ended and we returned to our seats. When I sat, Frank released his hold.

"That was lovely," Frank said as he patted my hand. "My childhood friend and sweetheart dancing. Now, play nicely, my love."

"Yes, darling," I muttered as the entrée was brought out. Before the waiter left, I stopped him. "Please take my plate and just bring me a glass of Blackberry Moscato."

"Yes, my Queen," he said and followed my direction without question.

"Is that how you know each other, Robert? You were childhood friends?" I asked, praying the waiter would make quick work of my wine.

"Yes, Your Majesty," Robert replied. "We both went to the Petrichorian Academy together."

My wine arrived and I sipped at it. "Did you run together?"

"You remember that, Rose?" Frank asked wistfully.

"Of course I remember that. It does not seem like ten years ago to me, Francis," I snapped.

Robert cleared his throat. "Actually, yes. We did run together, though Frank was always just a bit faster than me."

"Hmm." I drained my glass and indicated I wanted another. The waiter walked over with the bottle and refilled my glass.

"Were you in the Guard, too?"

"No, Ma'am. I was not built for it. Following orders has never really been my thing." I gave him a disbelieving look. "Alright – well – maybe for the revolution, but I have been well-rewarded for my hard work and obedience."

I swallowed the wine in two large gulps and lifted my glass for another. "So you have. With the best province Arboria – sorry – Milleria has to offer. Tell me, are we renaming the provinces, too, Frank?"

Not noticing my increasing calm and change in demeanor, Frank responded, "I have considered it. I am undecided on it for now. At the moment, all the provinces have retained their names and boundaries."

I drank half my glass. "I would recommend not changing the boundaries, darling. Things are confusing enough as it is."

"I agree with the Queen, Frank," Robert said. I did not care if he agreed with me or not. I finished my glass and raised it for another refill. Robert gave me a concerned look and I glared at him.

Who is he *to begrudge me the only way of surviving my marriage to this madman?*

I drained my fourth glass, then turned to Frank. "Francis, darling, I think I'm going to head upstairs now and get ready for bed. I'm feeling – *hiccup* – quite sleepy. Take yer time with yer friend." My words were starting to slur and I was sure I was completely sloshed.

"After four glasses of wine on an empty stomach, I am sure you *are* sleepy, Rose. Go ahead. I will see you later," Frank said.

"Please, take yer time." I turned to Robert. "Do not disappoint me, Robert." I said it both hoping he would keep Frank a long time and that he wouldn't ruin the province once belonging to my Father's brother.

"I will not, my Queen," he assured me.

I swaggered past the band with a wave of my fingers and Lucas gave me a sad smile. As I passed him, he sang the lyrics,

Follow the Hare through the looking glass,
My Queen of Hearts

But I heard nothing else. I thought it silly. After all, Alice followed a white rabbit down a rabbit hole, not a hare through a looking glass. The idiot was messing up Lewis Carroll big time and it angered me in my buzzed stupor.

"Is a white rabid, you – *hiccup* – idjut!" I yelled from the hallway and heard Frank laugh behind me.

When I stumbled into my room, Marie was waiting for me and caught me before I could land on the floor. "Blossoms, Mir – my Queen. You are drunker than a skunk."

I traced my fingers down her cheek gently. "Don judge – *hiccup* – me. If you were marry to a – *hiccup* – monster, you would exape reality, too."

Marie smiled. "I suppose you are right, my Queen. How many glasses of Moscato did you have tonight?"

"How'd chew know?"

"It is your favorite."

I scrunched up my face as I considered my glass count and saw her try not to laugh. "I think four glasses – I *think*. Giveortake."

"Well, let us get you cleaned up and in bed, huh?"

"Soundz good."

Marie allowed me to use her as a crutch over to the sofa, where she helped me out of my clothes, then washed me clean in a rose bath. After helping me into a nightgown and tucking me into bed, she turned to leave.

"Marie?"

She turned back to me and my drunk eyes filled with water. "Why?"

Any humor she had left her face as she came back to sit next to me on the bed. "I had no idea they were going to *kill* anyone. I would never have done that to you."

"Not an answer."

Marie sighed. "It was time for change. It began when High General Miller caught wind of the possible foreigners' King's Test. The whole palace was abuzz with it. I later learned that by the time the vote came through negatively, it was too late. The Nobles were already infected. Doctor Winston did his best to fix the problem, but he could not."

"So he really *did* feel bad."

"Yes. The fact that it was even *considered* for foreigners to compete for the Crown and your hand was outrageous to us. When I was asked to spy on you, I thought long and hard about it. I thought I was doing the right thing by not only the kingdom, but by you, even if you could not see it. I was wrong.

"I am here now, not for the revolution, but for you. I do not expect you to believe me or forgive me, but I hope to earn your trust again. I am sorry for the part I played in all this. Francis is a monster."

I said nothing as I processed her words and she must have taken it to mean I was done with her. Before she left, I stopped her again. "Marie, I forgive you." She smiled and left.

A while later, I felt Frank's moist lips on my shoulder when he crawled into bed. I pushed his face away with the palm of my hand. "Not *that* drunk, Francis."

He laughed and whispered, "Officially six days now."

Chapter 7

The days before Christmas went by like a whirlwind. I avoided the Throne Room like the Daze by running around the palace with Marie planning and decorating like a mad woman. Christmas was Mother's favorite time of year and I was determined Evergreen Palace would feel like she was there.

A couple times, I reminded myself of Alan Daniels and his idea about the trees having feelings. I found myself speaking to the trees of the palace more than once, out of sheer lonliness, but did *not* taste them.

Though Frank insisted he didn't like using his ability to control people, it certainly didn't seem to stop him using it on me now that I knew about it. The things he made me do were silly and stupid, like crossing my eyes or spinning in circles, but they all served as a reminder of what he could do.

I felt absolutely powerless. I had no visions. I couldn't pull Harrison into my dreams and it started to worry me into wondering if Frank had found him. The only comfort I had was that I was fairly certain Frank would rub it in my face if he had. He would probably kill him in front of me in the throne room. Or worse – make me kill him.

On Christmas Eve, I put on some gardening clothes and picked up the red tulip bulbs Marie ordered for me to go into my garden. It was time. I had sat with my garden planners and had them prepare the perimeter of the garden to plant the flowers.

As I planted them, I thought about how different life would have been had the mutated Daze never been. I thought of Stephan's smiling face and good humor. The way he protected me my whole life from any and all negativity.

"Come on, Stephan! You're going to love it," sixteen-year-old me says.

"I'm coming! I'm coming!" Stephan says, even though he is taking his time on purpose. Typical.

I turn around and grab his hand in mine and pull him down the glass hallway, stopping at the door.

"Close your eyes," I say.

"Really, Rose? It's a glass door. I can see it already. It's beautiful."

"No! Don't look yet!" I scramble to cover his eyes with my hands.

Chuckling, he says, "Alright! Alright!"

He closes his eyes and I take his hand again, pulling him in. I set him in the perfect spot. "Alright. Open them," I squeak breathlessly.

When he opens his eyes, he gasps. "Rose, this is – this is incredible. You designed this?"

I nod. "It's a maze! Come on!" I take his hand and giggle as I take us through the colorful maze.

"Ouch!" I hear him say.

"Watch out for the thorns!"

"Gee, thanks."

Finally we make it to the center of my rose garden and I plop on my sofa swing.

Stephan sits next to me and begins to swing us. "You really outdid yourself this time, Rose. This is amazing. I'm proud of you."

"Listen," I say and close my eyes. "Can you hear that? The sound of the rain on the glass roof? That's why I did this. It's so peaceful. I figure I'm going to need some peace if I end up married to Leonard or Christopher or Boring Brian."

"I thought Lincoln was on your negative list, too. And did you add Brian?"

I shrug. "Linc's not so bad. Just ambitious. At least he doesn't try to nonchalantly feel me up. And Brian has the personality of tree bark."

"What about Peter and Theodore?"

"I don't know them well enough to form an opinion. Honestly, Stephan, as weird as it would be, you are the only good option out of my possibilities."

Stephan chuckles. "Gee, thanks."

I look at him dubiously. "You know what I mean."

"Yes, I do. I will amend my previous promise. I promise I will do better than Leonard, Lincoln, Christopher, or Boring Brian, alright?"

I smile. "Alright."

The memory brought a smile to my face as I planted another bulb. I only had a few more left.

"I love seeing you smile, Rose."

Leave it to Frank to ruin a moment.

63

"This is kind of a private time for me, Francis," I said, the smile slowly leaving.

He came over and sat by me on the ground. "Please don't stop smiling on my account." I felt the slimy eel of his control slip into my facial muscles and a smile formed on my face unwillingly. "Didn't know if I could do it," he mumbled.

I looked over to him with the sweet smile he put on my face. "Well, now you do. Can you stop, please, and let me mourn?"

He released his hold. "You didn't seem to be mourning when I came in."

"Well, I was. It was just a happy memory I was having. Of when I brought Stephan here for the first time, just after the garden was finished." I planted another bulb, then grunted as I made another hole. "I was sixteen. He was twenty. It was before I knew Peter really well – why am I sharing this with *you*?"

"Because no one else is available?" Frank handed me a bulb and I nodded to him in begrudging gratitude.

"Yeah. That has to be it. Anyway. It was a couple of months before Peter and I started seeing each other secretly and we were talking about the participants in the King's Test." I planted the bulb and started a new hole. "Life was so different then. So much simpler."

"You talked about the King's Test with him? Wasn't he a participant, too?" He handed me another bulb.

"Yes, he was. And yes, we talked about it all the time. He was my best friend. Like a brother to me. Of course, a few days before he died, he confessed his romantic love for me." I set down my shovel and wiped the sweat from my brow. "By the time he told me, I had pretty much figured it out on my own. That first kiss interview really does teach you a thing or two. If there is anything I regret in life, it is that I didn't see it sooner. That we had no time together." I stuck the bulb in the ground and picked up my shovel to start another hole.

"So you knew he loved you when he died?" He handed me the last bulb.

I rolled the tulip bulb in my palm, remembering Stephan's soft lips in the kiss that took our whole lives to happen. "Yes, I knew. We would have been happy together, I think. He would have won the King's Test, I'm sure, had all the Nobles not died."

I gently placed the final bulb in the ground and patted the dirt on top. "For you, Lincoln," I whispered, kissed my fingers, and tapped the dirt. Frank had the sense to not say anything.

Standing up on weak legs, I took a moment to regain my balance and allow my blood to flow regularly. Frank stood, too. "You did good with those tulips, Rose."

I sighed. "What do you want, Francis?" I began to walk away and he grabbed my hand.

"I just knew what you were doing in here and thought I would check in on you. You have been here all day."

"It's a big garden." I looked down and didn't bother trying to take my hand back. Frank was obviously in one of his moods where he was going to try to convince me to love him or at least forgive him for what he had done to me.

"You are such a compassionate woman, Rose. How did I get so lucky to have you as my wife?"

"You killed everyone I knew and loved, and threatened to bomb my kingdom if I didn't marry you."

Frank pulled me into an embrace as if he hadn't heard me. He was quite adept at ignoring my barbs at his lack of humanity. "Grief is a double-edged sword, Rose. You hurt, so the people around you hurt, too."

"If that was true, you would have several broken bones by now."

"Oh. It's true, my brokenness is just not physical."

"I hate when you do that."

"Do what?"

"Talk all poetic. You're evil. You're not supposed to be eloquent."

Frank chuckled his stupid chuckle. "Do you see the full moon?" He pointed to the glass ceiling with one hand while keeping me close by the waist with his other. "There is not much that is lovelier than a clear sky on a winter's night."

Not until he said that did I realize I really had been planting tulips in the garden all day into the night. "What time is it?"

He shrugged. "It was around 9:00 when I came down here."

I rubbed a dirty hand down my face. "I need to get to bed. I have a long day tomorrow." Christmas. The Christmas party. What was to follow the Christmas party. I pushed Frank off me and walked out of my garden with him close on my tail.

"Lucas was concerned for you at dinner," Frank said.

"Oh, blossoms. We were supposed to practice, weren't we?"

"Mm-hmm. But I let him know where you were."

"I don't really care if he was worried about me. I am more concerned that I won't be able to rehearse before tomorrow night."

We made it to the room and Frank leaped forward to catch up to me before I made my escape to the bathroom. Wrapping his arms around me from behind, he said, "We can have a little rehearsal for tomorrow night right now, if you want."

He went to kiss my neck and I got away. Before sliding the bathroom door closed, I grumbled, "Nice try, Romeo." Frank chuckled as the door closed in his face.

I started the hot bath water and poured some rose oil in. After peeling my dirty, sweaty clothes off, I lowered myself in the tub and contemplated the predicament I found myself in.

What am I going to do? I need to give the rebellion more time. I cannot give myself to him tomorrow night, no matter what I said I would do. This is survival. I will have to fight him. There's no way around it.

Try as I might, I could come up with no way to do it, though. I couldn't even fight him forcing a smile on my face, how was I supposed to fight him forcing me to do the unthinkable. How horrible would he make it for me? Would he allow me to be unconscious while it happened? No. That would be worse.

After a bit, Frank knocked on the door.

At least he knocked this time.

"Everything alright in there? It's not safe to fall asleep in the bathtub," he said through the door.

"It's not safe for me here anyway," I quipped. With a deep sigh, I said, "Fine. I'll get out. Don't you *dare* come in here!"

Frank cracked the door open and placed a folded nightgown on the counter without looking.

"You forgot the underwear!"

"No, I didn't," he chuckled.

Pervert. I hate his stupid chuckle and his stupid face. I hate how he stupidly thinks he's so clever when he's really just stupid.

I pulled myself out of the tub, dried off, and pulled on the low neck, long-sleeved satin nightgown. He just couldn't wait. "Really? This thing barely covers my chest!"

"That's kind of the point, Rose."

I walked out with my hands covering myself and he did his stupid chuckle again from the bed with crossed legs. "I'm not wearing this," I said as I walked to the closet to change. I put on some underwear, day trousers, and a sweater, since all my concealing pajamas were hidden away somewhere. I had been wearing the long nightgowns, but he just *had* to push his luck.

"You're no fun," Frank pouted, frowning at my choice of attire.

"I'm not trying to be fun. I'm trying to make your life miserable. I could have sworn I made that clear a long time ago," I said as I pulled myself into the bed. A shiver crawled up my spine as I considered it would be the last safe night I would have in that bed.

"This nightgown will work just fine," he said as he pressed light kisses on my covered shoulder and up my neck.

"I still have one more day, Francis," I reminded him.

He groaned and nibbled at my ear, sending goosebumps up my arm. "I'm not going to try to take you. I just want to kiss you here." He nibbled my ear again. "And here." He kissed right under it and he turned me onto my back. When I tried to turn back, I felt his control slither under my skin and stop me. "And here and here." He kissed my throat and collarbone while roaming my waist and hips with his hands.

"Francis, release me," I breathed as he braced me between his arms and rubbed his nose against mine.

"In a moment. I just want a little taste." He pressed his lips against mine. His mind control forced my lips and tongue into a repulsive tango with his and he groaned with pleasure several times over the next few minutes as he forced me still and continued to run his hands over my body.

Finally, he ended his assault and released his hold on me. Quick as a cricket, I turned on to my side away from him and he followed me with a final kiss to my shoulder as he wrapped his arms around me. Nuzzling my neck, he whispered, "Just a reminder. If you decide to fight me tomorrow night, you won't succeed. I will have *all* of you. You *will* bear my children, my heirs."

I'm sitting in the back seat of the hover the Royals use to escort their visitors with High General Miller. He looks years younger and is giving me the evil eye. A memory? When was I ever in a hover with High General Miller?

"It isn't fair," I say, but it isn't my voice. Whose voice is this?

"Son, it is what it is," High General Miller says. Son? I recognize my voice now. I'm Frank.

"It is what it shouldn't be," I snap back with teenage boy angst. "Her life, if that's what you want to call it, it isn't fair. She has had to sacrifice too much!"

High General Miller gives a long-suffering sigh. "It's a part of being Royal, Francis. The King had to make the same sacrifices growing up. He had a Queen's Test just as Princess Miriam is going to have a King's Test, assuming there are survivors."

"What if there aren't?" I mutter the question.

"Then I suppose the Arborian Council will have their foreigners' King's Test," he says with a sigh of defeat. I don't know why.

We sit in silence until we get home. I turn to go up the stairs, but High General Miller places a heavy hand on my shoulder. I look him in the eyes and in them I see pride and anticipation.

"Francis, step into my office. I think it's time I bring you in on something."

I gasped out of the vision and Frank simply chuckled into my neck, probably assuming I was reacting to him. In silence, I laid there and waited until I heard the rhythmic breathing of sleep coming from him, stewing on what had just happened.

I had seen a memory of Frank's. That was new. If I wasn't mistaken, it was the car ride home from when he met me shortly before my freeze. It seemed as though that was the night High General Miller brought his son into the rebellion.

It was ironic, I thought, that what he perceived as the injustices of my life influenced him in his rebellion. He had taken more from me in the previous two weeks than society had in my lifetime. His rebellion took everyone I loved.

Was this a new part of my ability that I could learn to control? It could be beneficial if I could target specific memories. Before I could dwell too long on the progression of my abilities, I fell asleep.

I sit in my treehouse, afraid and trembling. Alone. I have been alone in my thoughts for too long. How I long for someone, anyone who actually cares for me to appear and give me some form of comfort.

"I'm here."

I turn to the familiar voice and cannot believe my eyes. "You can't be here. You have been dead for a long time."

The apparition laughs. "Of course I can be. This is your dreamscape and anyone or anything your mind desires can appear."

I reach out and touch the familiar face of Stephan. His grey-green eyes sparkle with humor. "Why you? I haven't dreamt of you before."

"Well, you spent a long time thinking of me today. And you need comfort. And I was your best friend."

Stephan puts his arm around my shoulder and I lay my head on it. I think of how unfair life really has been for me. Frank wasn't wrong all those years ago, but he hasn't done anything to fix it. He's only made it worse.

I believe in God. I believe He's in control, but I don't understand why He has allowed everything to happen. I need to think through it.

"Why does Frank have to have an ability?"

"I don't know. I'm only you. I won't pretend to understand God or why He allows the things He does. He did give us free will, though. Frank used his free will to give into the temptation his gift provided him. Just as with any gift or talent, humans are free to use them as they want. Although, it is important to remember that to whom much is given, much is required. There are many on your side with gifts that will come for you."

I lift myself out of the embrace and look him in the eyes. "You really think so?" Stephan nods with a smile. "Before tomorrow night?"

The humor disappears from his face. "No. Probably not before tomorrow night."

"Haven't I endured enough? I feel like life is too much. I have no one left. I would have thought Harrison would be there, but I can't even get him to come to me in my dreams."

"Perhaps he hasn't been asleep at the same time as you. Maybe he is preparing to save you."

"I know Frank has been trying to find him."

"It is time for you to wake up now, Miriam. Remember, you are not alone."

71

"No. It can't be time already. Please, don't make me wake up so soon."

Stephan traces my cheek with his finger. "You are not alone."

Chapter 8

For the first time in my life, I woke up Christmas morning with a sense of dread instead of joy. Pressing my palms against my face, I thought about the dream I had. I got out of bed and began pacing the room.

Alright. No one is coming today. But someone must *be trying. Harrison* has *to be trying. He can't have forgotten me. Why wouldn't he be sleeping at night, though? Is there anyone besides Louis and me in the palace still loyal to Arboria? How am I going to get myself out of tonight?*

Behind me, the door opened and I turned, expecting to see Frank, but it was Louis. "Is everything alright, Louis?" The door closed behind him and he searched every inch of the room, only to find nothing.

"You tell me. I know I heard you talking and there is not a holocomm in here. The secret passageway is guarded on the other side. Who were you talking to?"

I waved him off and continued pacing, putting my thumbnail between my teeth. "Just talking to myself, I guess. I didn't realize I was."

Appearing awkward, Louis asked, "Is there anything you want to talk about?"

I stopped and faced him. A pregnant pause sat between us as I considered whether or not to say anything. "I miss him. Harrison. I miss everyone I have lost. I saw Stephan in a vision last night and I think it has just gotten to me."

"My Queen, Stephan of Oak has been dead for many years."

"I know that!" I snapped.

"My Queen," Louis calmly walked over to me and gently took my hand. "I know you are nervous about tonight and I wish there was something I could do to stop it."

"The ball will be fine. I am not worried about it."

Louis cleared his throat. "I am not talking about the ball."

It took me a moment to figure out what he meant. When I did, I was outraged and humiliated all at once. "Roots! Does the whole palace know?!"

"It is all he has talked about with his lude friends any chance he gets. He also likes to rub it in my face personally because he knows there is nothing I can do about it without endangering you further."

Removing my hand from his, I shuffled over to the sofa and sat down. "How am I supposed to face all those people this evening when Frank has been talking about – *it* – to them all?"

"With the same dignity you have maintained so far."

I allowed that to soak in for a moment. Dignity? What dignity? I had essentially become a wino and put on airs of someone who doesn't care about anyone or anything anymore.

"Am I a good Queen, Louis? I feel so helpless. All my fighting seems to be for naught." I spoke softly and looked at my folded hands in my lap.

Getting down to a knee, Louis said, "You are a good Queen. The people know you have no respect for Frank and as long as they see that, they know there is a chance for Arboria to rise again."

Just as he finished talking, the door opened and Louis shot to attention. Frank stopped in the doorway and tilted his head. "What is going on here?"

"I thought I heard something unusual in here, Your Majesty, and came in to investigate. I found Her Majesty distraught and sought to –"

"– It is not your business to comfort the Queen, Louis. Please get back to your post."

"Yes, Your Majesty," Louis said as he left the room.

Frank walked over and sat next to me. I tried to scoot closer to the arm, away from him, but was already leaning against it. "Are you distraught, my love? It's Christmas day. A day for celebration." Frank reached over and took my hand and my lower lip trembled.

I didn't say anything at first and decided to try my new ability. Deciding to try something simple, I reached for a memory that we shared. The night he escorted me to my birthday ball all those months ago. It was easier than I thought it would be.

I stand in the hallway in front of Princess Miriam's room already sweating, but not because of the August heat. Tonight is the night I bring Rose to the island with me.

Without warning, the door to her room slides open and she steps out. My mouth goes dry. She's a vision in green and gold, with her neckline and arms fully exposed, with the exception of those gloves. Why is she wearing gloves during summer? Just when I didn't think she could become any more beautiful, she spins in a slow circle with a grin on her face. I can't help but smile back. When she notices my smile, hers widens and I quickly school my features. She can't know my feelings. Not yet.

"Are you ready, Your Highness?" I say to her. I follow behind her as we make our way to the Main Ballroom.

The vision flickered out. It worked, but I quickly had to remember his question. His expression didn't tell me any time had passed. Right. Something about my being distraught.

"I heard a rumor that greatly upset me because I know it can only be true," I half-lied.

"What rumor is that, Rose?"

Turning to meet his gaze, I said, "That you have been discussing what is to happen between us tonight with the noblemen."

Frank's face turned red. "Who told you that?"

"It doesn't matter who told me it. It can only be true. How else would my source know?"

"It's not like it sounds, Rose."

"Isn't it?" I took my hand from him and stood up, shaking with anger. "It's not you bragging that you are going to own the Queen of Arboria once and for all? It's not you discussing in grand detail what you intend to do to me? It's not you making sure everyone knows that we will be a real couple after this evening? It's not you boasting that your child will be within my womb?"

After a pause, he said, "Alright. Honestly, it *is* a little how it seems."

"Agh!" I walked away from him towards the bathroom in revulsion, but his slimy control stopped me when I was almost there.

"I said, it's a *little* how it seems. I am not going into any sordid detail with anyone. Promise. I have just been assuring them that the Royal line will not end with you and will continue with me. Tonight."

He released me and I turned to face him, still sitting on the sofa with his legs crossed in front of him. "How am I supposed to face all those people tonight, Frank?"

"You called me 'Frank'," he said with a smirk.

"You're unbelievable. Please leave so I can get dressed. I need to check on the decorations."

Frank folded his arms behind his head and leaned back against the sofa. "I'm not going anywhere."

With a sigh, I walked into the closet and chose an outfit for the day. Later on, Marie would come in and help me get ready for the ball. Much to Frank's chagrin, I got dressed into a pair of ivory trousers and a sapphire blue blouse *in* the closet, then ignored him when I left the room.

Louis in tow, I made my way down to the Main Ballroom and found Lucas and his band playing their instruments on the stage as decorating was well underway. Frank might have been an idiot, but his idea to hire a band for the palace was not wrong.

"Good morning, Lucas," I said when the song they were playing ended.

Lucas laughed and ran a bejeweled hand through his hair. "It is no longer morning, my Queen of Hearts. It is 2:00 in the afternoon."

For some reason, Lucas, his bandmates, and a few of the palace staff had taken to calling me the Queen of Hearts. I wasn't sure if I should have been offended to be compared to the fantastical queen infamous for beheadings or glad that I hadn't heard "Rose of Petrichoria" in a very long time.

"Blossoms! Why does Francis allow me to sleep so late?"

"Probably so he does not have to face the only person in the kingdom brave enough to talk back to him for part of the day," the bass player, known only as 'McGee' said. I laughed as Dawn, the drummer, ba-dum-chinged the drum set.

"You are probably not wrong, McGee." I shook my head, then walked around the room and teared up as I saw Mother's final ball plans come to fruition. In anticipation for dancing and revelry, the dancefloor was left open. Along the sides of the room were tables, decorated with mini evergreens and shiny green ribbons, and chairs for those less inclined to dance. The trees were adorned with copper and ivory glass, and spiraled white lights. The chandeliers had garland and holly on them, and every so often one, would find mistletoe hanging from the ceiling.

I closed my eyes and thought back to one Christmas long ago. A happy Christmas. My last happy Christmas.

"Dancing with you is the highlight of every Christmas, Rose," Stephan says.

"Only because you won't dance with anyone else," twenty-year-old me says back. "Honestly, I won't be offended if you dance with any of the other women. You know how pouty they get when you gentlemen won't dance with them."

Stephan laughs. "I never dance with them."

"Exactly."

"My turn!" Peter exclaims without a shred of formality at the end of the song, and sweeps me away from Stephan. I squeal and Stephan laughs good-naturedly.

"Pet – Count Peter! Put me down!" I laugh and have to correct my informality in public.

"You're gorgeous tonight, my love," Peter whispers in my ear as he sets me down and holds me close in a waltz.

"Thank you."

We dance in companionable silence for a time until Peter randomly stops in the middle of the floor.

"Why are we stopping?" I ask.

Peter looks up with his eyes and I follow his gaze to the mistletoe directly above us. "Your mother has really outdone herself this year, Rose."

Peter bends down and kisses me chastely on the lips.

"Your mother was a brilliant decorator, my Queen of Hearts," Marie said, taking me out of my memory. At some point, she had appeared next to me. "Rumor has it you have been standing here for quite some time."

"Hmm? I suppose that is possible," I mumble.

"Memories, my Queen of Hearts?"

"Yes. Good. I was thinking about my last Christmas before my freeze. With Peter and Stephan. Ella and I changed places dancing with them all night. It was one of the only balls I did not dance with Theo. It was a good night." I smiled.

"Indeed. If I remember correctly, much apple cider was consumed by you that night as well. You needed a lot of help getting ready for bed."

I laughed. "Cook was famous for that hard cider."

We stood together and watched as the decorators finished their jobs. Lucas and the band had finished rehearsing, which I apparently missed *again*.

"Shall we head up to get you ready, Queen Miriam?"

"What time is it?"

"4:00."

I shot her a look. "I have been standing here for two hours?" As I shifted my weight, I realized it was true. My whole body was stiff from standing in the same position for so long.

"No one blames you, my Queen of Hearts. It is a difficult day for many of us."

I nodded. "Very well. Let us go."

We turned and left the quiet ballroom behind. As we climbed the stairs to the fifth floor, I was greeted by a few of Frank's Nobles with "Merry Christmases" and "We are *so* looking forward to this evenings." A couple of the Dukes looked at me with lecherous, knowing looks and I wanted to stab their eyes out with stakes of holly.

When we entered my room, I had finally stopped referring to it as my parents' room, Frank was starting to get ready as well with his assistant, Mark. Before I could say anything, Marie spoke up.

"Your Majesty, would you mind so much if Her Majesty got ready in her old suite? We will need more space than is allotted here with you preparing as well."

"Yes, yes. That will be fine. I will see you in a bit, my love," Frank said dismissively and without a hint of hesitation.

Quickly, Marie went to the closet, grabbed the dress and we left before Frank could rethink his agreement. When we entered the room, I noted the holocomm sitting there and looked at Marie with wide eyes.

"Quickly. There is a message on there for you. Check it before Frank realizes he sent us in a room with one."

I rushed over to the holocomm wondering who could have left a message or who would have even known it would have been possible at the moment. Pressing the button to play the message, I stilled and waited.

Up popped Harrison's handsome face and I began crying immediately. "Oh, Rose," he sounded apologetic. "I wish I was there now. I have a source who has told me Frank's plan for you tonight. There is no way to get you out of there in one piece or it would be done. I know you have made life difficult for him and I know you will continue to do it."

He sighed and ran his hand down his face. "The thought of his hands on you – I will kill him. I know you won't make things easy for him, even with his ability. Yes, I know about it – now. Everyone does. There are plans in place, Rose. You are not alone. I can't say all who is with you because I don't know what kind of resources Frank has – for all I know he has a mind-reader like me. But it is safe to say the one who brought you to this message is with me.

"I love you and will get you out of there as soon as I can. Be brave, my Queen of Hearts."

That was the end. His face disappeared and the message automatically deleted. To know he was out there trying to get me out made me so happy, I nearly forgot about the horrible night I had ahead of me. Almost.

Chapter 9

Two hours later, I was standing in front of a full-length mirror with a giant deep-red dress and comfortable ivory shoes on. My long black hair was down, with a few braids throughout it and my mother's – no – *my* Queen's crown sat atop my head for the first time.

I had always admired it from afar. The tiara was large, but not gaudy, with emeralds and diamonds woven in a floral design. I had barely a moment to look at myself in the mirror when Frank came into the room, dressed in an ivory suit with a blue vest. Upon his head sat a large crown laden with sapphires; it was not Father's crown, something for which I was glad.

He eyed me beginning at my toes and ending at my crown. Pressing his lips together, he turned to Marie, "What is this?"

I quirked a brow at her, not knowing what he meant. "My lady is quite lovely, is she not, Your Majesty?" Marie asked with feigned innocence.

"Quite," he said sternly. "However, this" he pointed at the crown on my head "is not the crown I gave you to put on her this evening."

Marie stepped over to examine the tiara. "Blossoms. Silly me. This is Queen Amoura's tiara. I must have grabbed the wrong one when I gathered Her Majesty's outfit for the evening." Delicately,

Marie removed my mother's tiara from my head and winked at me so Frank couldn't see. "I will be right back, Your Majesties."

As Marie quickly left the room, Frank brought his attention back to me and stepped towards me. He paused when he noticed the holocomm. "I trust you made no comms out while you were in here?"

"Of course not. Who would I comm? Everyone I love is dead."

"Not *everyone*, Rose." I tilted my head in question. "Not Harrison."

I laughed. "And how would I go about comming Harrison? I don't have his comm address in Southland. Besides, do you honestly think I'm stupid enough to make any comms at all on a holocomm that is likely being recorded?"

"Come now, Rose," he said, now close enough that he could pull me to him by my waist. "You have to know by now that he isn't home."

"How would I know that, *Francis*?" Even after two weeks, I still enjoyed the silent victory of seeing his eye twitch and jaw clench. "I have had no communication with the outside world for weeks."

"Hmm. I suppose you're right. Just so you know, though. If he steps foot on palace grounds, I will personally see to it that he is killed. No. I will see to it that *you* kill him."

That's what I was afraid of.

"I under – "

"Here it is, Your Majesty!" Marie burst into the room and Frank jolted away from me.

"Please, put it on her. We are running late now," Frank said.

"Yes, Your Majesty," Marie said. I noted that she never called him "my King" or "King Francis" and that made me smile as she placed the white gold crown, with sapphires and diamonds among golden roses, upon my head.

"Much better, my love," Frank said, taking my hand. "Let us attend to our guests." He kissed my hand and escorted me from the room without another word to Marie – or allowing another word from me.

As we descended the stairs, I tried to think of ways to separate myself from him. I looked to each branch, hoping for a lack in security, but found it not lacking, but doubled. That meant all the secret passageways were blocked. They had probably even found my super-secret one in my garden by now.

I silently cursed the fact that he had been my personal Guard for a time. Only the Royal family was aware of *all* the secret passageways, but their personal Guards knew about most of them. While Frank had clearly not given away the locations of all the passageways he knew about, the branches where they were located were well-guarded.

As we approached the Main Ballroom, Frank stopped and stood in front of me. For moments, he just stared, like he was trying to memorize my face.

"What?" I asked, perturbed and just wanting to get everything over with.

"Just remembering another moment in time when you actually *wanted* me to escort you into a ball," he responded. That seemed like another lifetime ago, not only a few months ago. Back when he was Frank, my night Guard – the one entrusted to protect me from harm. Before he became the greatest traitor in the history of Arboria.

"That was a long time ago, Francis," I responded, breaking eye contact.

He tipped my chin back up so I was looking at him. "Not too long."

"Long enough. We were both different people then."

Frank couldn't argue that. He pressed his lips together, nodded stiffly and looped my arm into his. In the next moment, the guards opened the door to the Main Ballroom and we were greeted with applause and music. Frank smiled and waved and I brought a forced, small smile to my face.

I was there because it was Christmas. I was there to take part in the last thing Mother ever planned. I wasn't there to make Frank proud. And I wasn't there to represent anything he did.

As we descended the steps, I noticed the same leering faces as earlier. Leaning over to Frank, I whispered, "I refuse to dance with *any* nobleman you spoke with about tonight. Do you understand? They are making incredibly rude faces at me."

He stood straighter and looked out as if trying to see what I saw. He must have because he leaned into my ear and said, "Very well. I will have conversations with them privately about their behavior as well. Though I do expect you to dance with Duke Robert of Maple."

I looked to find Robert and he was smiling nicely. "Fine," I muttered.

We came to a stop at the bottom of the stairs and Frank held his free hand up to silence the gathered Nobility.

"Welcome to our home for the first annual Royal Millerian Christmas Ball!" Frank proclaimed and the crowd cheered. Once they quieted, Frank continued. "It has been a long year – a difficult one for us all, but we have come out victorious in the end.

"Tonight, we celebrate the birth of our Lord –"

Hypocrite.

"– and the sacrifice He made to save us all. Our very own Queen recognizes sacrifice and I hope you all look to her as an example of how you should be as leaders of your own provinces."

I closed my eyes and counted to ten, trying to not ruin Christmas night, but unable to stop myself from being offended at Frank's comparing my sacrifice with that of Christ. Seriously. If he thought of me so highly, it was no wonder he was so "in love." However, his plans for the rest of the evening did not reflect such lofty thoughts on his part.

"Cherish the loved ones you have and remember those you have lost. We will take a moment of silence to do so now."

The air of the ballroom was thick in the demanded silence that followed. I was certain everyone present could feel the tension and righteous anger rolling off me in waves. Every word from Frank's mouth was an insult to my family and me – really for all of Arboria. He had even declared the event the Royal "Millerian" Christmas Ball!

After a few uncomfortable moments, Frank finally broke the silence. "To begin our evening, Queen Miriam will join the Royal Millerian Band in some songs she and lead singer, Lucas Flowers collaborated on."

Oh. I'm opening. Just grand.

As I floated my way across the room to the stage, one nameless Duke whistled and another catcalled. "That is enough!" Frank shouted murderously. I paused in my path, shocked at the outburst. "Duke Sandran of Sequoia and Duke Michael of Elm step forward. My Queen, return to me."

All three of us approached Frank warily. I was tired of his posturing, but they looked genuinely afraid. Frank wrapped an arm around my waist when I neared his side. To the noblemen, he asked with menace, "Who is this woman?"

The men eyed each other as if arguing mentally who would dare speak. Duke Sandran lost and said, "Queen Miriam, my King."

"What is she Queen of, Duke Michael?"

"Um – Milleria, King Francis."

"Tell me, is she your Queen? Do you serve her? Desire to give her honor and respect?"

"Yes, Your Majesty," Duke Sandran and Duke Michael said simultaneously.

"Then bow and apologize for your abhorrent behavior."

The men did so and I nodded in acceptance.

"Dismissed," Frank said and the men scuttled back to their terrified and embarrassed wives. "Let this serve as a warning to everyone present. This woman is your rightful Queen and is deserving of your respect and honor. Should she receive anything but that from any Noble, their family will be stripped of their Noble title and they will be banished from Milleria. Understood?"

As one, they said, "Our King declares the truth!"

Banishment? Holy wow!

Rather than send me over on my own, Frank walked me over to Lucas that time and gave me a hand onto the stage before rejoining the crowd.

Backs facing the crowd, Lucas mouthed, *Are you alright, my Queen of Hearts?*

I mouth back, *Yes.* We couldn't speak at all or the amplification bar lining the stage would pick up our voices – even the slightest whisper.

The set we collaborated on consisted of three ancient Christmas carols. Knowing the music for most of the evening would be upbeat and modern, I selected somber songs – it was how I was feeling, after all. We opened with *O Holy Night*, then did *The First Noel* in a minor key, and closed with *Silent Night*.

I could have played my guitar, but I didn't feel like sharing too much of myself with the people before me. Lucas stepped back and harmonized to my melody. A sacred hush fell over the crowd when we began and I could almost feel a tinge of guilt flow from several people. Several servants had tears in their eyes and some guards swayed subconsciously to the slow rhythm.

Lucas' baritone seeped into my soul and I felt like I had in the rose garden during his interview when he sang to me. Not that I wanted him to kiss me – that his voice affected me. Every anxious and nervous thought left my head until all that was left was the music and our voices joined in blessed accord.

The siren was at work in my mind again and it didn't even bother me. I needed it – needed something to drag me out of my melancholy and bring a sense of peace, even if it was only for a little while.

When we finished, no one made a sound. The noblemen, noblewomen, servants, and guards were equals in that moment of actual, uncommanded silence. Looking around at the crowd, I *knew* they were finally remembering all those people who had died over the last two weeks and ten years ago to prop them up in status.

Men held their wives, who cuddled into them with contemplative looks on their faces. Frank even looked a bit taken aback. Before anyone could ruin the silence, the emergency holocomm dangling from the ceiling lit up.

"People of Arboria!" The head of a beautiful blonde woman appeared. She spoke with a similar accent to Harrison.

Who is that?

"I am Queen Natalie of Southland. I have heard of the tragedy taking your great kingdom by storm and offer aid. Should anyone from Arboria decide to seek refuge, you will find it within our borders until power is restored to rightful rulers.

"To Francis Miller, your atrocities have been noticed not only by my kingdom, but by others, as well. Should you decide to continue your charade as King, aid will come to the people of Arboria in the form of my army and the armies of our allies. We align ourselves with Queen Miriam, whom you hold captive. You have three days to surrender. I await your comm."

With that, the beautiful Queen Natalie's face faded out. Not sure what to say, I stood with my mouth agape along with my bandmates.

Frank chuckled nervously and pulled at his collar. Feeling brave once again and pulling myself back together, I grinned and spoke to my audience. "Long live Queen Natalie of Southland!" I wished I had a glass of wine in the moment so I could have made it a toast. Lucas cough-chuckled behind me.

Frank cleared his throat. "We will discuss this later, my love."

"Anything, *Francis*," I said as I offered him my hand to help me from the stage. Jaw clench. Eye twitch. Inner victory dance. Another cough-chuckle from Lucas.

"Ladies and gentlemen, let the festivities begin!" Frank shouted, blatantly ignoring the threat from Queen Natalie. I liked her already. I didn't recall ever meeting her before, but she seemed familiar. That was probably due to how much she looked like Harrison. She appeared to be in her mid-twenties, with Harrison's blue eyes to match their similar blonde hair.

Before I could think any further on my possible future sister-in-law, Frank spun me around into position for The Rose and Lucas' band played my famous waltz to begin the dancing.

"If you had wine in your hand, what you said could have been construed as a toast to the woman that just threatened our kingdom," Frank whispered in my ear.

"It is funny you should say that. When I was finished, I briefly longed for a glass of wine to do just that," I retorted with a giant grin.

"So, you are alright with someone straight out saying she will invade our kingdom in three days?"

"No. Not *my* kingdom. Didn't you hear? She offered aid to *my* kingdom. In fact, it sounded like she had backup as well. It is only a matter of time before she declares checkmate on you, Francis."

"This changes nothing about later tonight."

"It changes *everything* about later tonight."

The song ended and Duke Robert cut in without a word to Frank and swept me away as another song began. He smiled wide as if he knew Frank was left flustered when he pulled me away.

Maybe I was wrong about him.

"Your voice was spectacular tonight, *my Queen of Hearts*," Robert emphasized the title in a telling way and I knew he was actually with Harrison. My eyes widened in surprise and his smile grew bigger.

"Uh – thank you, Duke Robert. It has been a long time for me. I was glad for the opportunity to perform."

We spent the rest of the dance in smiling silence, and the rest of my evening was spent being passed from Duke to Duke to even a couple servants and guards. It was as if there was no coup and Queen Natalie didn't comm. Life was celebrated that evening.

But every celebration must come to an end.

Chapter 10

My final dance of the evening was with Louis. It was an upbeat, jovial number in 4/4 and the first time I had seen Louis truly smile in ages. When the song ended, we laughed as we tried to get our rapid breathing and heartrates under control.

When I felt familiar arms drape themselves around me from behind, my smile quickly fell from my face and Louis rejoined his place along the wall. I was able to get my breathing under control by taking deep breaths, but my heart was racing a mile a minute.

"It pains me to say this first annual Royal Millerian Christmas Ball must come to an end. We have enjoyed your presence this evening. For those of you traveling, be safe. Merry Christmas!" Frank orated.

"Merry Christmas!" everyone repeated.

Frank switched positions so he was leading – actually, he was sort of pushing – me by the small of my back towards the exit of the ballroom. I glanced over to the band and saw Lucas give me a solemn nod. The rest of the band mimicked his gesture and a tear fell from my eye.

No one will be coming for me tonight. This is my *fight alone. It is up to me.*

I tried not to notice Frank's odd gait as we ascended the stairs, knowing it was due to his – um – excitement for what he thought was to come. Knowing I had told him I would give myself to him tonight, I dreaded the fight to come.

Frank would be angry at my defiance and I wasn't sure what kind of fight he would bring to the table. Oh. I was positive he would use his ability to try to get what he wanted, but I felt empowered myself. Between the promise of assistance from Queen Natalie and the calm brought on earlier in the evening during my performance, I felt I just might stand a chance in keeping his slithering control at bay.

"You are dismissed," Frank said coolly to the guards as he shoved me into the room.

"Your Majesty?" one questioned.

"You *dare* question me?" Frank shouted at him.

"Of course not, Your Majesty," the other said and yanked the first one away towards the stairs.

As soon as I saw them leave, I ran for the bathroom. The door slid closed and I locked it before Frank had a chance to take hold of me.

"Rose, there is no point in defying me. You told me you would give yourself to me tonight," Frank said with a contrived layer of patience as he approached the door.

"No!" I yelled at him.

Frank tapped on the bathroom door with his fingertips. Still calmly, he said, "Come on, Rose. Unlock the door."

I felt it then. He wasn't going to try to convince me; he went straight for the jugular. The snake of his control went for my hands. Before I could even think to fight it, my hand reached out and pressed the button to unlock the door.

Grinning widely, he cooed, "Step on out, Rose. Our first time will *not* be on the bathroom floor."

Like a marionette, my legs brought me out of the bathroom, past him, and to the middle of the floor. I felt like my arms were glued to my sides. Frank was in total control.

He stepped in front of me, and I watched my hands reach out and remove his suit jacket and begin unbuttoning his vest. "Please, Frank. Don't do this," I begged.

"Ah. I love it when you call me 'Frank'."

"Please."

"Hush now, Rose. There will be no more negotiations," Frank said as my hands slid off his vest and made quick work of the buttons on his dress shirt.

I tried to beg more, but found my mouth forced shut. My eyes widened. He told me he had no control over whether someone spoke. As if reading my thoughts, Frank corrected me. "I said I couldn't control whether someone gave me information I wanted or not. Not that I couldn't prevent someone from speaking at all."

After my hands removed his shirt, they fell like lead to my sides again. Slowly, Frank made his way behind me and pushed my hair over my shoulder and undid the buttons on my dress, letting the bodice fall to my hips. As he began undoing the corset, I began fighting his control even harder and felt a finger twitch.

It's possible!

"Would it be *so* bad, Rose? To give yourself to a man who adores you? Who loves you? Who would move Heaven and Earth for you?" He pressed a kiss to my neck just below my ear. "Just give yourself to me. Let me love you and I will be your slave."

Fight. Fight, Rose.

Just as the thought occurred, I slipped into another of his memories.

We sit on the sofa of the second room Rose has been in since being at the island. I was so nervous, I chugged my wine.

I have her wrapped in my arms and we've been reminiscing about our past. It's kind of funny now in a weird way, how we've come from being separated so far by rank to being equals.

I can't take my eyes off her. So beautiful. So mine. I kiss her.

I gasped at the end of the memory. It was so disorienting seeing myself like that and hearing his thoughts. I forgot to fight for a moment and my legs went out from beneath me. Frank wrapped his arms around my body to catch me as the dress and corset separated from me. He cradled me in his arms and I stared at him in horror as we approached the bed.

Fight HARDER!

Something snapped then. I felt a thick liquid trickle from my ears, eyes, nose and mouth. Blood. Frank stopped moving and said, "Stop fighting me. I don't know what it's doing to you."

My whole body began to tremble as I pushed even harder to fight. Pretty soon, I was no longer trembling, but shaking. Frank gently tossed me onto the bed and my shaking turned to thrashing.

Finally, I felt his presence leave my mind, but it was too late for me. Eyes rolling up into the back of my head, I began seizing and bleeding more. "Rose!" I heard Frank's muffled shout just before I blacked out.

I wake up in the arms of Peter, being held closely to his bare chest. Wait.

"Peter! What are you doing in my bed?" I shout at him as I jump out and take in my surroundings. There is a window on one

wall and it is snowing. A wooden fence tells me I am in a room on the first floor of some building that is not Evergreen Palace.

Peter just watches me as I look around. The bed has a green quilt and sits between two nightstands. Mine has what appears to be an archaic communication device, connected to the wall with some kind of cord, and sitting on top of it.

"Peter, what's going on?"

With hands open in a reassuring gesture, Peter sits up. "I'm not Peter. I'm David, remember? This is our bed."

"David?" I wrack my brain, trying to remember who he is. "Uh – husband? From my false life, right?"

"Right. See my eyes?"

Cautiously, I rejoin him on the bed and look into his eyes. Not brown. "Blue," I murmur.

"Yes. David," he says, placing one of my hands on his chest.

"David," I breathe.

"You're unconscious. I thought maybe being here might be reassuring for you."

"I'm unconscious? Why?"

"You fought Frank with your mind and it gave up."

"Roots," I swear.

"It's not a bad thing. Well, it's not a particularly good thing, either. But you stopped him from getting what he wanted."

"But I'm unconscious."

"Yes."

"Roots."

"Yeah," David runs a hand through his hair. "Just lay back and relax, Miriam."

"Relax," I mutter as I do what he says. "Why am I so tired? I'm not usually so tired in my dream world."

"Like I said, you fought hard. You're tired, inside and out." David pulls the quilt up and tucks it around me as if he is swaddling me.

"I'm tired. I'm repeating everything you say, it feels like."

"Technically, you're repeating yourself," David whispers as he gives me a kiss on my forehead like he is going to disappear.

"Don't leave! I'm scared. I don't want to be alone," I slur hurriedly, unsure that he actually understands me.

"Of course I understand you, Miriam. I'm you. I'm not leaving." David lays down next to me again and places a strong arm over me. As my eyes close in my dream world, I hear him say, "I'm not going anywhere until you don't need me anymore."

Part II

Chapter 11

Beep. Beep. Beep.

The distinct sound of medical equipment greeted me when I came to. I was still in my own bed. Gingerly, I turned my head to find Frank fast asleep next to me – not touching me. On my other side, I found Doctor Quincy asleep in a chair.

At least I'm no longer alone with the beast.

My body felt rooted to the bed and it took work to lift a hand to rub my eyes. Unfortunately, the movement woke Frank and he wrapped an arm around me.

"Ugh," I grunted with displeasure, not only because he touched me, but because my tender abdomen clenched when his arm rested on it.

"You're awake," he said in a raspy voice that told me he had been crying.

"So it seems. Thanks for putting clothes back on me," I whispered sarcastically with my tired voice. Rather than being naked like I was when I passed out, I was in pajama pants and a long sleeve shirt. I hated losing time. "How long this time?"

"A couple hours," Frank said quietly, still cuddling against my broken body, and ignoring my bristly mood and sarcastic quips.

"I need to use the bathroom," I whispered. Frank tensed. It was a crude thing to say, but I needed to. I tried to move my legs to get up, but couldn't. My legs weren't responding to my mental demands to move. "Frank, why can't I feel my legs?" I whispered in a panic.

"You had a stroke, dear," Doctor Quincy said as he stood from his chair and checked my vitals.

"A what?" I whispered, horrified. I gave Frank a pathetic push off me, which he allowed. "This is *your* fault!"

Frank stroked my head gently as he sat up to try to placate me, but I had already begun crying. "It's alright, my love. You can be fixed. You will walk again."

Doctor Quincy snorted and Frank gave him a dirty look. "Don't sugar coat it, Doctor," I whispered to him. "Tell me how it is."

Doctor Quincy put his Note-Taker down on his chair and sat on the edge of the bed next to me. "Poor Miriam," he said, I thought somewhat to himself. "You have been through so much. I am truly sorry this has happened to you."

"It is 'Queen' Miriam, Doctor," Frank said obstinately.

"You can call me 'Miriam,' Doctor. Please continue," I corrected and Frank frowned.

"Thank you, Your Majesty," Doctor Quincy said, clearly amused. "Your body wasn't capable of fighting as hard as you were against His Majesty's mind control." Doctor Quincy bravely gave Frank a disgusted look and Frank looked away. "Essentially, you gave yourself a stroke since your mind was where the battle was taking place.

"Your stroke has taken your ability to use your legs. I can fix it with a minor brain surgery, but I will need to shave your head and it will take a day of recovery for your legs to be useful again."

Medical miracles of our current day.

Because it is something I do when I am nervous, I spouted off a random fact about the twenty-first century. "Could be worse. Back in the twenty-first century, someone would be lucky to get feeling back at all, much less after only a day. Recovery could take weeks, months, yea –" Frank interrupted my tirade by taking my hand and I looked at him. I was so angry. He released my hand after seeing my look.

"Will you assent to the surgery, my Queen of Hearts?" Doctor Quincy asked quietly.

I looked back to him and nodded.

"You can make use of any room on the premises for operating, Doctor," Frank said.

Doctor Quincy sighed. "I am afraid I will need to bring her to the hospital, Your Majesty. There is not anywhere sanitary enough on palace grounds – not since the lab was burned to the ground."

Frank grunted. "Fine, but she will be guarded round the clock. Understand, Doctor?"

"Of course, Your Majesty."

"And I will join her in recovery."

"Francis, I don't think you will fit on the bed with me in the recovery room if it is the same one I woke up in after my freeze," I pointed out in a hoarse whisper, hoping I could dissuade him, but knowing I couldn't.

"Then get a new bed put in, Doctor," Frank demanded.

With a heavy sigh, Doctor Quincy said, "Very well, Your Majesty."

Doctor Quincy left to make arrangements and Frank took my hand again. Out of everything that I had been told, the most superficial thing stood out to me. "All my hair," I whispered with a tear and he squeezed my hand.

It was silly. I had won. I defeated Frank at his own game! I was still whole. I would get my legs back and hair grew, but it was my *hair*. My crowning glory. And it would be gone probably within the hour.

"Rose – " Frank started.

Because I had no use for his platitudes and apologies, I interrupted him. "Please ask Marie *nicely* to have several head scarves made for me. She will need to be sure they coordinate with my outfits."

Frank gave me a pained expression, but nodded and left, hopefully to do as I asked, then sulk around feeling like the monster he was. If he was a different person, I might feel bad for making him feel worse, but he was Frank. He felt bad now, but that didn't mean he wouldn't be trying for my womb again when I healed. He would just regroup and come up with a new strategy to get into my proverbial pants.

I had been away from him before then, but without the use of my legs, I was stuck wherever I was brought. Whether I was stuck there at the palace or at the hospital, it didn't matter. I was stuck. I hated being stuck. I was *really* beginning to hate blacking out and hoped that after my surgery, there wouldn't be much more of it in my lifetime.

Glaring at my blanketed feet, I tried to shake my hips. Yup. I could use my hips. Thighs? Nope. Knees? No. Shins? Nuh-uh. Feet? Not even my toes. I growled.

This sucks.

After what felt like an eternity, Doctor Quincy and Frank returned with a hover gurney, medics, and Louis along with them. "It's about rotting time," I pouted, knowing I looked and sounded ridiculous with my hoarse whisper.

Louis smiled and I could tell he was amused at my attempt to appear intimidating and relieved that I had succeeded in my venture to stop Frank from getting what he wanted. "Glad to see you awake, my Queen of Hearts," Louis said as he helped the medics lift me onto the gurney.

"Where did that title come from anyway?" Frank asked absentmindedly.

"What title?" I asked.

"Queen of Hearts. Wasn't she in some fairytale or something?"

"Yes. She was the evil queen in the book *Alice's Adventures in Wonderland* by Lewis Carroll. Please tell me you have read the book or seen some version of it in film or theater, Francis."

"I have not. Is it in our library?"

"Of course it is," I snapped as the medics began making the uncomfortable descent down the Core. It was unnerving on the gurney.

"Then I'll go grab it quickly before we leave and read it to you during your recovery."

"Fine," I muttered and he took off. "Might as well grab *Through The Looking Glass*, too!" I shouted after him.

"Anything, my love!" Frank shouted back.

"Idiot," I muttered. Doctor Quincy, Louis, and the two medics laughed. "Oh. This is funny now?" I questioned, my voice gradually returning to me.

"Not at all, my Queen of Hearts," Medic One said. "Though I will assure you that as far as rumor has it, your title has not been given to you because she was evil in the story."

"Is that so?" I asked.

Medic One nodded. "Indeed. It is because of her ferocity and the people's willingness to do as she commanded without question. One major difference, though, is that people obeyed her out of fear. Your people follow you because they love you, my Queen of Hearts. That is another reason for the name: you are Queen of all our hearts."

I smirked as we exited the building and Frank rejoined us. "Found them, my love," he said.

"I hope so! No one should be even *thinking* about touching my classic literature without my knowledge!" I grabbed his hand as they brought us onto the ambulance hover. "You haven't been letting people touch my books, have you? I will have your head if you have."

"Off with his head!" Louis said, unable to contain himself and everyone, but Frank, laughed – he didn't get it.

"No one has been permitted entry to the library except you and me," Frank assured me.

"Good. Make sure it stays that way."

As we took off to the hospital, I felt slightly happy, able to forget, at least for the moment, that I was about to have my head shaved and cut open. Oh. And Frank was still King of *my* kingdom.

Chapter 12

In the operating room, I became nervous again. Frank had tried insisting on being present for the operation, but Doctor Quincy resolutely refused, much to my delight. I always loved seeing someone stand up to Frank and get away with it – it did not happen often.

"You may be King of Milleria, but in this hospital, I am in charge," the Doctor had courageously declared. "I have had a larger bed brought to the recovery room. You may wait for her there. This discussion will go no further." Then he slid the door to the operating room closed in Frank's stupefied face.

"I like you," I said to Doctor Quincy as he approached my side and the anesthetic began to work.

"That is good, considering I am about to cut open your head," he responded.

"I'm sorry I thought you were a villain," I said seriously, but it must have sounded funny because Doctor Quincy laughed. "Seriously. You're not a villain." I yawned. "You're my hero."

"I am glad to be of service, my Queen of Hearts. Now sleep," he said sweetly, like a father would. And I did. I slept soundly through the whole operation.

I sit on a bench, drinking in the totally fake sunshine and loving every minute of it. Everything around me is in my head and I know it. Does it bother me? Not at all. If there is anything I have learned over the last ten and a quarter years, it is that sometimes a mental escape is just what I need from the real world.

In this world, I can do whatever I want. Those evergreen trees in the distance? Boom*! Everpurple trees. Blue skies?* Boom*! Pink skies. Hungry?* Boom*! Blackberry tart. I think I may need something to wash it down.* Boom*! Blackberry Moscato.*

My real life is filled with all kinds of things I cannot control, even though I am the Queen. Queen? Psh. In name only. No one cares to listen to me. No. That's not quite *true. There are apparently loyalists within the palace that would listen to me if I asked something of them. However, they are incognito, so I have no idea who they are.*

Harrison does. I wonder if Harrison knows about all the loyalists or if some of them have just joined lone-wolf style. Because it is a different time of day than I usually sleep, I wonder if I can get a hold of Harrison now. When I dreamed of Stephan, he had thought perhaps the only reason I was unable to bring him to be before was because he wasn't sleeping at night.

I briefly think of Harrison. Closing my eyes, I think of his Kona-blue eyes and true blond hair. I think of how tall he is and how I have to get on my tip toes to kiss him. I think of his brilliant smile and the look he makes when he reads a stray thought of mine. Next thing I know, I'm being pulled up into large, laughing arms and swung around in circles.

"Rose!" Harrison yells in triumph, as if he is the one who brought us together.

"Harrison!" Admittedly, it is cliché that these are our first words to each other, but I am so excited to see him, nothing else comes to mind, except that I really need to kiss this man I love. So I get on my tip toes when he sets me down and I do.

I tilt my head back and gently tug his head down and our lips meet and dance in that oddly familiar way. Harrison pulls me tight against him and whispers into my hair. "I have been so worried about you."

"I've been worried about you, too," I whisper back just before he captures my lips again.

"I'm so sorry about your parents – and Phineas. I should have listened to you."

"It's not your fault. No one listened to me. In the end, I didn't even believe those doubts myself. He's long gone anyway. Probably angry with Frank because I banned him from the palace. Frank had him staying in my old room."

"Your old room?"

"He moved us into my parents' room."

"Us?" He looks like he wants to rip something apart.

"What did you expect? I had to literally get on my knees and beg for him not to take me that first night." I pause. "I was so scared and thought there was no one left when Adele fled the palace."

"I'm so sorry I wasn't there for you. With time zones and traveling, the work to save Arboria is best done at night."

I look up at him again. "Is that why you haven't been sleeping at night?"

He quirks a brow at me. "How can you possibly know I haven't been sleeping at night?"

I shrug. "Deduction. I haven't been able to bring you into my dreams for the last several nights. Plus, Stephan told me."

"Stephan?"

"Long story." I proceed to tell him everything. About the events leading up to the wedding. About my memories returning. About Frank's horrible torture and murder sessions. About Stephan and everything he had said to me.

We pause our conversation and I just let Harrison hold me as he lets everything I have said sink in. "Can you tell me who in the palace is with us?"

"Oh!" He squeezes me a little tighter with his reluctance. "I wish I could tell you everything. But I still don't know what kind of people Frank has surrounding him. Have you seen a mind-reader at all?"

"I don't think so. But I have met some unlikely allies of mine."

"Who? I don't want to give anyone away."

"Marie. My old assistant who was a traitor. And Robert Casey. That was a real shocker. Do you know his story?"

"Not entirely. I know he wasn't with us until after recently having dinner with you and Frank. Frank had used his ability to force you into dancing with Robert and it was the last straw for him. He couldn't believe Frank would use that ability on the woman he claimed to love."

"I thought I saw something change in him that night."

We stand there for several minutes, just holding each other. Finally, Harrison asks, "Why are you asleep right now?"

"Oh – uh – you don't know yet?"

He holds me back at arm's length. "Know what?"

"So – Frank tried to – you know – last night."

"Even after Natalie's warning?!"

"Yes. I fought his mind control. Hard. Too hard." I sigh. "Harrison, I gave myself a stroke and lost the ability to use my legs. Right now, I'm under anesthesia and Doctor Quincy is performing brain surgery on me. I'll be in recovery for a full day before I will be able to use my legs again."

"You're in brain surgery *right now!?" He exclaims.*

"Yeah."

"Shouldn't your brain be taking it easy or something?"

I laugh. "Doctor Quincy didn't say anything about it, not that he would know to do so, though. I'm just relieved to know I can still do this. I was concerned I had destroyed this gift when I had the stroke. Frank still doesn't know about it, so this rendezvous will go completely under his radar."

At first, he's upset, but then, his face lights up. "I have an idea. Oh! A brilliant idea! I wish I could tell you." Harrison kisses me. "I have to go prepare. I love you. I will see you soon, Rose."

"I love you too," I say and he leaves.

I retake my seat and recline under the sun for the remainder of my surgery. Soon, Harrison and I will be back together. And together, we will retake Arboria from Frank.

"'Oh, you can't help that,' said the Cat: 'we're all mad here. I'm mad. You're mad.' – " True to his word, Frank was reading *Alice's Adventures in Wonderland* when I woke up. He stopped there for a moment and muttered, "This is complete nonsense."

"That's kind of the point, Francis," I whispered. "It's a children's story. Nonsense makes children happy. That's why Wonderland was so wonderful. It was straight from the imagination of a little girl."

"I'm glad you're awake, Rose," Frank muttered. "But a grown man wrote this book."

"From the perspective of a child."

Frank set the book down and pinched his nose as if trying to ward off a headache. I breathed a laugh. "Is it really that bad for you to read a book out loud?"

"Maybe I should just find a film."

I laughed quietly as he crossed the room to a holocomm that wasn't in the room during my first stay. He ordered someone on the other end to locate the film, then turned around to lean against the holocomm desk with his legs and arms folded. He stared at me.

"What?" I asked, feeling a little nervous at the perceived anger I saw in his gaze.

Frank unfolded his arms and slapped his hands on the holocomm desk at his sides. "I'm sick and tired of this, Miriam!" he shouted.

Here comes the temper tantrum. I knew it was only a matter of time.

"You called me 'Miriam'," I said quietly. Frank had to be pretty upset to be calling me by my real name.

"Yes. I did," he said in a not-soothing quiet voice. "You keep getting yourself hospitalized with your stubbornness."

Rolling my eyes, and trying not to let him intimidate me, I lay my head back on the pillow and looked at the ceiling. "I choose to look at it as *your* stubbornness that keeps getting me hospitalized. I only had that hunger strike because *you* refused to send me home. And I only had the stroke because *you* forced yourself on me."

Next thing I knew, he was at my side, hovering over my face. "Listen to you. Pathetic. What has your fighting gotten you?" He paused a moment at his rhetorical question. "Pain! Death! Loss of *everything* you care about – including your lovely hair!" Frank shouted and spittle flew in my face.

I frowned at him. "Are we seriously having this discussion right now? I'm recovering from brain surgery, Francis!"

Jaw clench. Eye twitch. Slap! I squealed.

Didn't see that coming.

"It's 'FRANK' for you! You will call me 'Frank' from now on! Every time you call me 'Francis,' I will slap that smug fight right off your face! Am I understood?"

Rubbing my reddening cheek, I whispered, "Yes, Frank."

Frank turned my head to the side stiffly, then pressed a soft kiss on my burning cheek, his lips catching the fresh tear that fell from my eye. He lowered himself to sit on the side of the bed and embraced me as I trembled from weakness and fear.

In my ear, he whispered directly into my ear, "I do not like punishing you, Rose. But I have had quite enough of this. If I have to slap you every now and then to prevent you from ending up back here, I will do it. I love you too much to watch you kill yourself. I am at my root's end."

He pulled back and made me look him in the eye by holding my chin. "I will promise you this. If you continue to fight me on the consummation of our marriage, I will simply have you drugged and take from you what I desire. It's not the way I want it, but I will take what I can get. You are mine. I will have you. Do you understand?"

He's crazy.

I swallowed hard and whispered, "Yes, *Frank*."

Frank smirked at the use of his name and traced a finger down my reddening cheek and pressed a soft kiss to my lips. He whispered, "I love when you say my name."

As if he hadn't just slapped me across the face and completely blown his lid, he asked, "How are you feeling? I know how much you hate losing time."

113

"I hate that you know that," I muttered, either idiotically or bravely – or a little bit of both. "But I think I'm alright. A little tired, ironically."

Aside from the sting on my face, you nut-job!

"Doctor Quincy said you might be and it would be alright for you to spend a lot of your time during recovery sleeping. You've already slept through most of the recovery period. You have about eight hours left. Then, we can try using your legs. I have a surprise for you when that time comes."

"Oh goody," I mumbled.

"You'll like this one," Frank promised, then kissed my forehead.

"Ugh. I'm going back to sleep."

Frank chuckled as I turned onto my side – the not-reddening side of my face – and began to doze off again, back to my own, personal Wonderland.

Chapter 13

When I came to again, Frank was reading *Through the Looking Glass* with the same frustrated look on his face he had earlier when he was trying to figure out Lewis Carroll. I stayed quiet and closed my eyes again, not wanting to alert him to my consciousness.

Though I had hoped to reenter my dreamscape, my sleep had been dark. It was one of those times when I fell asleep and woke up, feeling only moments have passed, when I knew it had actually been hours. Seeing Harrison earlier had been nice, though it felt as if the visit reopened the old wound of being separate from him.

I sighed without thinking about it and Frank asked, "Are you awake now, Rose?"

Knowing he could tell if I faked it, I said, "Yes, though I wish I wasn't."

"Are you ready to try standing?" he asked, ignoring my jab.

Shaking my legs and wiggling my toes, I said, "Yes. I can give it a try."

Sitting up, I draped my legs over the edge of the bed. Frank gingerly took my hands, belying his earlier violent outburst, and helped me onto my weak legs. Before I could collapse, he let go of my hands and caught me by the waist. Quickly, to get his heavy mouth-breathing off my naked head, I pressed my feet firmly into the floor and assured him that I was alright.

Hesitantly, he moved his hands from my waist back to my hands and led me across the room to the holocomm desk. "Great job, Rose," he muttered encouragingly. "Now, it is time for your surprise." He carefully released one hand and pressed an address into the holocomm.

Lucas' face popped up. "Yes, Your Majesty?"

"We are ready, Lucas. Play away," he said. Then to me he said, "Let's dance."

"Dance? I can barely walk!" I protested as the song began and Frank pulled me in close.

"I'll keep you standing," he breathed.

The band began playing a slow song, and Frank began swaying us to the beat. After a couple measures of instrumentals, Lucas began singing.

> *Let not your mind*
> *Be troubled, my spark*
> *Let not your heart*
> *Be captured by dark*

Frank's eyes became half-lidded and his shoulders relaxed as he began to circle us and I thought he might be getting ready to kiss me.

> *For I am here*
> *Oh do not fear*
> *For we are here*
> *To save you*

Frank sighed dreamily and the swaying rhythm he had us in became slow and no longer in time with the music. Suddenly, the lyrics clicked in my brain and I shot a sidelong glance at Lucas' band on the holocomm, who then went back and repeated the same verse and chorus in a loop. Looking back to Frank, I saw he had not noticed, but was closing his eyes.

Next thing I knew, Frank's arms dropped to his sides and he fell to the floor, sound asleep. My legs shook and I caught myself on the holocomm table to prevent my fall. The door to the room slid open and Doctor Quincy came rushing in.

"What –" I began to ask.

"No time to explain. Let's get out of here before he wakes up," Doctor Quincy said sharply as he wrapped an arm around my waist to let me lean on him. With Doctor Quincy practically carrying me, we left the room. No one interfered with our fleeing. In fact, as we passed people in the lobby after descending in the elevator, they quietly smiled and bowed.

A hover van awaited us right outside the door. Without ceremony, Doctor Quincy opened the door and quickly pushed me in. Inside, Lucas was behind the wheel and the rest of the band was in the back with me, along with Louis, who was buckling me in.

Doctor Quincy began to close the door. "Wait!" I shouted. "Aren't you coming?"

Taking my hand, he looked me in the eyes. "I must stay behind, my Queen of Hearts. I confess, I am not completely innocent in all this. I helped Doctor Winston develop the mutated Daze all those years ago and have been trying to make amends since then. I will stay behind and continue to provide information to you."

"What will you tell Frank when he wakes up?" I asked quietly after Doctor Quincy's revelation.

"That is for me to worry about. Now. Go. Save our kingdom," Doctor Quincy ordered as he released my hand and closed the door. As he turned and casually walked back in the building, tears filled my eyes in concern for what would become of him.

The engine screeched as Lucas slammed on the accelerator and took off. I looked around the hover van at everyone in slight bewilderment. They all looked mightily pleased with themselves. "How?" It was all I could say through the shock of my rescue.

"The band was set up in a room on the bottom floor at the hospital," Lucas said, as if that answered every question.

"But – *how* – Why did Frank fall asleep like that?"

Lucas laughed. "Oh, my Queen of Hearts. You have not figured it out, yet? My voice holds power over people."

I gasped. "You *are* a siren! I thought I was imagining things."

Lucas frowned and Dawn laughed. "I do *not* have fins," he insisted, which made Dawn laugh harder. He sighed. "Although the ability is similar to a siren, I suppose. Weren't they all ladies?"

"I don't know. There had to be men, right? How else would they reproduce?" I said, in wonder that we were seriously having this conversation.

McGee choked on a laugh and Louis shook his head. "What?" I asked?

"We are having a conversation about how mythological beings used to reproduce as if they really ever existed," Rage, the violinist, offered with a straight face. Blake, the keyboardist, who didn't say anything ever, nodded his head in agreement.

Lucas huffed. "Just because there isn't any physical proof, it doesn't mean they never existed."

His bandmates sighed and Louis muttered, "Here we go."

"It's the same for a lot of things. Sasquatch. The Yeti. Chupacabra. You just never know."

"I do," muttered Rage with his head between his hands. Blake blew a hard breath through his mouth. I had a feeling they had this conversation a lot and only felt a little bad for being at fault for the conversation. I needed some levity.

"Where are we going?" I asked to change the subject. Plus, I really *was* wondering.

"The capital of the Sequoia province," Dawn replied. "To Loyalist Headquarters. It will be quite a drive, so you might want to just go to sleep."

For a few minutes, I really tried to fall asleep, but something was plaguing my mind. "Lucas?"

"Yes, my Queen of Hearts?"

"If you had this ability to control people with your words, why didn't you rescue me sooner? Why wait until after damage had already been done?"

There was silence while he seemed to contemplate an answer for me, then he spoke with a choked voice. "When we were asked to come to Evergreen Palace for an audition to become the Royal Musicians, I was already in communication with Prince Harrison. Many of us past contenders in the King's Test had contacted him, assuming he was going to lead some sort of rescue.

"I told him about the audition and suggested I do just what you said. I wanted to rescue you right away. After a lot of deliberation, we decided you were safe for the time-being, and as musicians, we would often be overlooked when private conversations were being held. It was the perfect opportunity to have spies on the inside.

"Also, your presence in the palace was big for morale for the nation. As long as you were residing in Evergreen Palace, there was hope. Without you, we were afraid people would give up.

"As Christmas approached, we went back and forth on what to do. Should we blow our cover and rescue you? Should we change Frank's mind?" Lucas sighed, then continued in a heavily apologetic tone. "We decided to choose the people. I valued the information and the faith of the nation over your well-being, and for that, I will never forgive myself. It was I who convinced Harrison to not move forward with a rescue attempt.

"I figured you would cunningly put him off again. Frank's obsession with you was ridiculous. He was so gentle with you compared with everyone else, even when he *was* using mind-control on you. I overestimated his care for you and underestimated the consequences of you fighting him off.

"When you had the stroke, Harrison was beside himself, and so, so angry with me. If he had been there in person, I swear he would have punched me in the face, at the very least. Then, we found out you had been transferred to Davidson Memorial, a place overrun with loyalists, and put a plan to save you into action. I'm sorry. I know that's not enough, but I will spend the rest of my life in service to you, trying to make up for what I did."

"We all will," Dawn murmured.

Leaning my head, dizzy with all this new information, against the window, I considered everything that was said. Part of me wanted to stay angry with Lucas and the band forever. How dare they make such assumptions and decisions based on those assumptions? How could they allow all that to happen to me?

Dawn, who was sitting next to me, looked extremely remorseful. When Lucas was speaking, I could tell by his voice that his decisions would haunt him for a long time, if not for the rest of his life, and I wagered it was the same for everyone in the van.

Reaching out to hold Dawn's hand, I said, "It will take me some time to move on from this, but I understand you were in a difficult position. All of you. Thank you for rescuing me in the end."

"I only wish we would have done it sooner," Lucas said darkly. "Try to get some rest now, Queen Miriam. We have a long drive ahead of us and you're still recovering from surgery."

With nothing more to say, I nodded and closed my eyes in an attempt to finally get some sleep.

Chapter 14

Sleep? Yeah right.

Sleep was impossible. Quite possibly, it was the furthest thing from my mind at that moment. Being the farthest point south in the kingdom, Sequoia sat at the border between Arboria and New California. Though it was hours of driving, I couldn't sleep a wink the whole way.

A billion thoughts ran through my head. Not the least was the curiosity of whether or not Harrison would be there. When we met in my dreamscape, it sounded like he was heavily involved in, possibly in charge of, the mission to retake Arboria. If he *was* in charge, I would be so proud. He would have definitely proven himself worthy to be King of Arboria in that case.

Also, I was thinking about what I would say to the people who had remained loyal to my family despite the insanity Frank unleashed on my kingdom. What could I say to inspire them? Running a hand over my bald head, I wondered if I was even still worthy of being their Queen. I couldn't even keep the kingdom out of Frank's control.

As I considered this, I sighed and watched the trees zip by outside my window.

Would Father have done any differently than me?

True, I married Frank, but it was under duress. Frank had said there were bombs planted all over the kingdom.

Was it true? Were they still set?

Southland certainly felt I was worthy of the Crown. I had to wonder how much of that was only because of Harrison and how he felt about me.

Does Southland only support us so Harrison gets a Crown? I wonder if there really are other countries allied with them to help us?

I wondered how long Frank would remain unconscious and how long it would be before he put out an ultimatum for me to return. Or even if he *would* let it be known that I was gone. If the people knew that I was no longer at the palace, would it embolden them to stand up to him? I almost hoped not – I didn't want anyone else dying.

He will never let me go.

With everything Frank had gone through to not only ensure he took the Crown, but me as well, I sincerely doubted he would just give up. Somehow, we needed to stay a step ahead of him.

As I was thinking about Frank, the holodash flipped on, and Frank's voice sounded throughout the hover.

"People of Milleria, I will keep this short and simple. Our beloved Queen Miriam has been kidnapped from Davidson Memorial Hospital during her recovery from surgery."

"Roots," McGee muttered over the announcement.

Frank continued. "She is being transported in a white hover van, and her head has been shaved because of the procedure she underwent. If you see or hear anything suspicious, please contact your local city guard. Should anyone give information that results in the return of Queen Miriam, you will be rewarded greatly. Thank you and have a good night."

Night?

During my musings, I must have at least closed my eyes because at the mention of night, I opened my eyes – not that it helped much. Besides the light of the waxing moon, there was no other light. The dim illumination from the slight moon and billions of stars shone on the surface of the vast and violent Pacific Ocean.

We had been driving too long for us to be in the Willow province, so I was guessing we were in the Sequoia province now. We had to be near the border. The thought made me wonder if Harrison had gotten the President of New California to join in our fight.

"Well, we're rooted," McGee said matter-of-factly.

"Not necessarily," Louis said.

"I think I'm going to be sick," Dawn muttered as she rolled down the window.

The breeze blew over my bare head and sent a shiver down my spine. I felt a hand on my shoulder and glanced over to find Louis holding out a green scarf. I gaped at him and graciously accepted it. While the melee of freaking out continued around us, Louis smiled and said, "I thought you might need it."

As I tied the scarf on my head, I quietly said, "Everybody calm down."

Though I wasn't sure how everyone heard me, silence fell, and Dawn rolled the window back up with an apologetic smile.

"No one is going to turn us in," I said simply.

"She's right," Lucas piped in from the front seat. "His description of the hover van was vague and we're not far out from where we're going anyway."

"Where *are* we going?" McGee asked with his arms crossed.

I looked over to him. "You don't know?"

"No. Only Lucas knows. For security reasons."

"Exactly," Lucas said. "Which is why I *still* can't tell you anything, McGee."

McGee huffed and dramatically tossed himself back against his seat. I glanced over to Dawn with a crooked eyebrow and she rolled her eyes at his theatrics. Rage just laughed out loud while Blake smirked next to him.

"I don't know why no one else is curious as to where we're going," McGee pouted.

"Oh, we're all curious –" Dawn began.

"We're here!" Lucas announced as he lowered the hover van into the middle of a beach.

Granted, it was dark, but as we all looked around, there was nothing particularly special about our location. It was a typical, freezing, northwest coast beach. There were no other hovers. There were no buildings. Nothing.

"Uh – Are you sure?" McGee asked.

"Yup. Just sit back," Lucas said with a smug grin, shutting off the hover. He pulled his hands up behind his head, and leaned back against the headrest.

So, we waited. Dawn and I played with my scarf to find interesting ways of putting it on my head. McGee, Rage, Blake, and Louis played some self-invented card game, which led to some ridiculous arguments – mainly between Rage and McGee. It was McGee's game and he was clearly changing the rules to suit him as they played.

As they bickered about whether or not the Queen of Hearts was superior to the Ace of Hearts, I leaned forward and tapped Lucas' arm. When he looked at me out of corner of one eye, I asked, "Aren't you concerned for the tide? We're just sitting here on a sandy beach and the waves are pretty crazy."

Lucas sniffled and said, "No worries, Your Majesty. The tide doesn't come up this far."

Just as I was about to ask how much longer we would be waiting for whatever it was we were waiting for, I felt the hover van lift, even though it wasn't on. Sand blew away from us on all sides and revealed a doorway, which opened, beneath us. Slowly, we were lowered down.

"Here we go, my Queen of Hearts. Down the rabbit hole," Lucas said with a grin.

When the doorway closed above us, we were plunged into darkness. Being blind in the pitch black, the sensation of being lowered consumed me. Breaths of everyone in the hover increased in speed and my heartbeat thudded in my ears.

"How deep are we going, Lucas?" I whispered into the apparent emptiness.

"Ten stories, Your Majesty."

"That's deep," McGee stated with an audible gulp.

"Uh-huh. The facility is beneath the ocean floor here, so it has to be."

That was when it clicked for me. I knew exactly where we were. Each province had an underground military base. The People's Base locations were only known by the elected officials. The Royalty and Nobility had their own underground bunkers in case of emergency. The separation of powers is what kept the People's Bases secret from Nobility and the Noble Bunkers secret from the elected officials. Why Frank had never asked me about the locations of the People's Bases, I had no idea, but I was glad he hadn't.

"This is the Sequoia People's Base, isn't it?" I asked.

127

Lucas smirked. "Very perceptive and smart, my Queen of Hearts."

"Is everyone here?"

"No. The Delegates from each Province are running their own People's Bases, but this is the hub. Every action the resistance takes is run through here."

"Is Harrison here?"

"He goes from base to base, but I'm pretty sure he's here now, waiting for your arrival."

At hearing that Harrison was probably there waiting for me, a giant smile spread over my face. After what felt like forever, the hover van finally stopped in a small, dimly lit landing room. With an absurd amount of exuberance, I flung the back door of the hover van open and hopped out, forgetting that I was still weak from the surgery and had yet to walk completely on my own.

"Whoa there, Queen Miriam," Louis said as he raced out behind me and caught me before I fell on my face. "Prince Harrison can wait a moment longer for you."

"Yes, but can I wait for him?"

With a light laugh, Louis held me out at arm's length so I could get my balance. With a sharp nod from me, he offered me his arm and we stepped away from the hover van so everyone else could get out.

The landing room was small, only big enough for the hover van and walking space to get out. The walls were plain, except for a shut metal door on one side. When I approached it and pressed the button to open the door, it chimed at me, but didn't slide open.

"What is this? Why didn't it open?" I asked out loud to myself.

"Queen Miriam Petrichoria recognized," the door said to me in an automated female voice, and slid open.

I quirked a brow at Lucas, who came to stand next to me. "Prince Harrison felt the need for extra security with everything going on. For your voice, we just found some old holocomm recordings of you giving speeches. Follow me, Your Majesty."

I mouthed "oh" as Lucas stepped out in front of me and began leading us down a white hallway. It reminded me of the hallway I saw shortly before waking up from my freeze. At the thought, I stopped in my tracks and my eyes widened.

I remembered something from my false life.

"Are you alright, Your Majesty?" Louis asked. Giving my head a swift shake to pull myself together, I looked up at him, then gestured for us to continue with my hand. Lucas had paused for us and proceeded down the hall when we were ready.

As the six of us passed people, they stopped and hastily bowed when they got over their shock. Although, I wasn't sure if they were more surprised by my presence at the Base or my lack of hair. Both situations were certainly shocking for me, so I couldn't imagine how it must be for everyone else.

Will Harrison still think I'm beautiful without my hair? Will he still want me, even though I'm weak?

We stopped at the fifth door on the right, and Lucas unceremoniously pressed the button to open the door and walked in. The sight that greeted me was most unexpected. Every single one of my Arborian suitors, aside from Lucas and Robert Casey, sat at a very large table with the Delegates of Arboria, even the Willow Delegate. At the head of the table, on the far end of the room, was Harrison.

Every face in the room turned to look at us when we entered. Lucas strode straight to Harrison, but the rest of us stopped just beyond the threshold, and the door slid shut behind us. As Lucas bowed, he said, "My Future King, I have completed the mission you set before me." He stood straight and addressed everyone in the room. "Ladies and Gentlemen, may I present Queen Miriam Petrichoria."

After only a slight hesitation, probably due to my unexpected arrival, everyone at the table stood and applauded. A couple yelled, "All hail the Queen of Hearts!" However, much to my relief, they did not yell it in unison – had they done so, it would have been unsettlingly similar to Frank's army of drones shouting, "Our King declares the truth!"

As everyone clapped and yelled, Harrison rushed around the table at full speed and dragged me up into his arms. Spinning me around in circles, he kissed me all over my face, muttering words of happiness and gratitude to God for delivering me to him safely. When he stopped spinning, he lowered my feet to the ground and kissed me soundly.

He still loves me.

The relief I felt must have poured into Harrison, who pulled his face away and cupped my face in his hands. "I heard your thoughts in the hall. I don't care if you have hair or not; you will always be my true love. No matter what."

"I love you," I whispered into his ear over the din of the room.

"I love you, too," he whispered back before giving me another kiss.

I meander my way down the stucco halls of Southland Palace.

"Hello, Prince Harrison," I hear and look in the direction of the flirty female voice. Lady Quinn twirls a blonde curl around a finger. Ugh. Not again. "Got a moment?"

I don't slow my stride. "Nope. Sorry, Q. I have a meeting with my sister. Can't keep her waiting."

I ignore the pout she gives me and hurry my pace. That woman just won't give up. None of these simpering ladies will and it's driving me tumbleweeds. It's not that I don't want to be married. I just haven't met the right woman. That woman is definitely not Q.

Elbowing the button to open the door, I wink at the guard stationed outside Nat's office and plop down on the chair on the other side of her desk. She doesn't even look up.

"You're late. Again." She's annoyed. Again.

"I don't see how I can be. We didn't actually have a meeting scheduled."

She looks up from her computer desk and gives me a dirty look. "I sent for you hours ago, Harrison."

I shrug. "I was busy."

"Doing what?"

"Sleeping."

"Ugh. When are you going to start taking yourself seriously?"

I decide to ignore the introduction to that conversation and eyeball the basket of fruit on her desk. "Can I have an apple?"

Nat throws her hands in the air in exasperation. "Sure. It's your basket. That's why I called you here."

I grab a big red and yellow apple from the basket and take a bite. Mmm. Juicy. Had to come from Arboria. "You could have just sent it to me."

"No. It came with a request. I wanted to be here when you saw it." Nat pushes a button and, sure enough, King Aaron of Arboria's face shows up on her holocomm.

"Greetings, Prince Harrison. As you may know, my daughter, Princess Miriam has been in a freeze for nearly a decade as scientists here and around the world have worked on a cure for a mutated version of the Daze with which she was infected.

"We have found a cure and will be picking up where we left off so many years ago with her Crowning Coronation and a King's Test. Unfortunately, there are no eligible Arborian nobleman of her age, so we are reaching out to kingdoms we trust that have Princes who qualify. You qualify.

"We would be honored if you would come participate in this generation's King's Test. It is the first that includes foreign participants, so you would be making history. Please find the details attached to this message and contact me should you have any questions. Thank you for your consideration."

The holocomm message pops off and I can't help but stare at the empty space. I look at Nat, who is amused.

"You cannot be serious, Nat."

"Serious as a twister at noon."

I throw the half-eaten apple at the basket and the contents spill all over the floor. "Our Royalty has always valued choice, Nat. It's why you aren't married yet. Do you know what the King's Test is? It's essentially the medieval practice of competing for the maiden's hand in marriage! You would arrange this?"

"No. That's why I'm giving you the option of whether or not you go." Nat leans forward on her arms and I can tell she's about to go into social manipulation-mode. "Princess Miriam is beautiful, Harrison. Not only beautiful, but she is famous for her graciousness and bravery. Look what she did for her people. Those are all qualities I know you're looking for."

Despite her obvious game, Nat's not wrong. Princess Miriam is a legend for following in her ancestor's footsteps. She may not have been as flashy as he was when he saved the world, but she did it nonetheless by isolating herself into quarantine to prevent the spread of that mutated Daze. The fact that it took ten years to come up with a cure seems to only verify how horrible the world would be if she hadn't succeeded.

132

Not to mention that Arboria is notoriously isolationist, with the exception of their lumber and fruit trade. The fact that they are opening their borders to allow for a foreigner to not only live there, but possibly marry to the Crown is history in the making.

My charming sister taps on the attachment, and it shows a tentative schedule of events, a contract that I will probably have our attorneys read, and a holo of Princess Miriam herself.

Blowing sands, she is gorgeous. What could it hurt to participate? What are the odds that I'll win some archaic competition anyway?

"Alright, Nat. I'll go."

Harrison had no idea what I had just seen, but I smiled big at him anyway. His "why not" attitude about the King's Test amused me greatly. I would share my new gift with him later on.

Turning back to face the table, Harrison held his hands out in a "calm down" fashion. When the room quieted and everyone took their seats again, he said, "This is great news, indeed! We will call this meeting to close and get some rest for the night. Tomorrow evening, we feast!"

The Delegates and Arborians stood and talked amongst themselves as they readied themselves to leave the room. When everyone else but the band, Louis, and I had left, Harrison gestured for Lucas to come over.

Lucas bowed. "Yes, Prince Harrison?"

As soon as Lucas straightened, Harrison punched him in the jaw without a word. Dawn yelped and rushed over to a fallen Lucas, who was rubbing the lower half of his face, nodding.

"Yup. I deserved that."

The two men stared at each other for a few more moments while we all waited in awkward silence. Finally, Harrison, sighed and softened his tone of voice.

"Excellent job leading this mission, Lucas. I never doubted you could complete it."

"Thank you, Your Highness," Lucas said as Dawn helped him up.

Harrison frowned at him. "I hit you, and I'm sure you've been mentally beating yourself up for a while now. It was my choice as well as yours." Harrison put a hand on Lucas' shoulder and bent a little to meet his eyes. "We're alright. That's enough of the formality, Lucas."

Lucas sighed, then said in an overly cheerful voice, "Thank God. I hate being all stiff around you."

My jaw dropped at the apparent comradery between the two men. I had known they were working together, but had no idea they were so familiar with each other. Harrison chuckled at my thought.

"Roots. I missed being in your head, Rose," he said with a humored glance at me. "Lucas and I became good friends during the months we were in the palace while you were away." *In Frank's captivity* went unsaid. "He has been instrumental in obtaining vital information from the inside and your return, as I'm sure you can now see."

"Yes, I now see it," I said dimly at the reminder that he was there watching my tortuous last few weeks the whole time.

Clearing his throat, Harrison asked, "Lucas, can you get Louis and your friends settled into rooms?"

"Louis is our friend, too," McGee said, patting him on his back.

Louis smiled, but said, "Thank you, but I think I would like to contact my family if it is all the same to you, Your Highness."

"Yes, of course. Do you think you can handle it, Lucas?" Harrison asked.

"Yeah, sure," Lucas said as if Harrison grew up down the street from him instead of in another kingdom as a Prince. "Follow me, mates," he said with a fake Pacifican accent.

"That was horrible," Dawn said.

"Aw. You know you love it, love," Lucas said with a peck on her cheek.

"Please," she said with a giggle trying to push him off, but he tickled her. I hadn't even known they were together. It must have been a recent thing, considering he had just competed for my hand in marriage not long before.

"Ugh. Come on, Lucas. It's late and I know I don't only speak for myself when I say I don't want to watch you two make out right now," Rage complained. Blake nodded his agreement.

"Alright, alright." Lucas released Dawn from his tickling fingers and chased her out the door. The other men grumbled as they followed them out.

Harrison and I stood in silence and stared at the door after they left. He took my hand in his, then kissed it. "Shall I show you to your room, my Queen of Hearts?"

Chapter 15

As Harrison and I walked hand-in-hand to my room, my mind spun over everything that had happened in one day. I had recovered from brain surgery. I escaped Frank's captivity for a second time. I rode for hours in a hover van to the Sequoia People's Base. I was reunited with Harrison.

I wanted to be angry with Harrison for the decisions he made based on Lucas' reporting and opinions, but I was just so relieved and thankful to be with him again, my heart couldn't take the ache of resentment and fury.

When my thoughts strayed to the horrors of Frank, Harrison squeezed my hand. "Breathe, Rose."

Taking a deep breath, I leaned into him and closed my eyes, allowing him to lead me blindly. If there was anyone I trusted, it was Harrison. Even though I had no idea what exactly he had planned, just knowing that he had *something* planned made me love him even more than I already had.

I couldn't believe how quickly I had fallen for him, and vice versa. Some might have said it was foolish to give my heart away so fast. Under most circumstances, I would have to agree. However, with Harrison always in my mind and our dreamscape escapades, I felt like I had known him for years.

"We're here, Rose," Harrison whispered into my scarf after a while. I opened my eyes and yawned as he was reaching forward to press the button to open the door. The sight nearly caused me to cry.

All the furniture from my parents' room, that I thought was gone forever when Frank remodeled, had been moved there. The dark wood and forest green materials greeted me like old friends.

On the bed lay one of my green long-sleeve night gowns. Again, I thought everything green from my wardrobe was long gone when the nation's name and colors had been changed.

Tracing the satin with my fingers, I said quietly, "I can't believe you got all of this. How?"

When I turned to look at him, Harrison was leaning in the doorway with a smug grin on his face. "Marie," was all he said.

"I hope she'll be alright at the palace," I said.

He walked toward me and the door slid shut behind him. "Don't worry about Marie. She'll be alright." Harrison cupped my face in his hands. "You just rest. We have a long day tomorrow before the feast in the evening. Good night, Rose." After a chaste kiss on my forehead, Harrison turned around and walked toward the door.

"Wait," I said. Harrison stopped and looked back at me. I walked up to him and took his hands in mine. My heart was beating loudly in my chest and I couldn't look him in the face. Quietly, I said, "Marry me."

He was silent for so long, I didn't think he heard me, so I looked up at his face. Since his eyebrows were raised to his hairline and his mouth was slightly open, I assumed he had, so I said nothing and waited for his response.

Squeezing my hands a little and clearing his throat, he said, "Rose, you know I want to marry you. I want to spend the rest of my life with you. We'll get married."

I shook my head, "Tomorrow afternoon, before the feast."

"Tomorrow?"

I nodded.

"I hate to say it, darlin', but you're married to Frank right now. Everyone who was watching their holocomm a couple weeks ago saw the wedding."

I scoffed. "That mockery of a wedding performed by that mockery of a pastor only created a mockery of a marriage. As far as I'm concerned, I'm not really married to Frank. How could I marry a monster like that?"

With incredible calm, he said, "You did it to save your people. There's no shame in that, Rose. And while it may be an event you greatly regret, it still happened. I *will* marry you, but we need to take care of your marriage to Frank first."

Even though I knew he was right, I hated hearing it. More than that, I hated Frank. I hated Frank more than I hated anyone in my entire life. With a growling roar, I spun around on my heel, stomped toward the bed, and began punching the pillow. Every curse word I ever knew flew from my mouth, and pretty soon my rage turned into wracking sobs. When I finished punching and slid to my knees, Harrison knelt next to me and brought me into his arms.

"It isn't fair," I cried.

"It isn't. He'll pay. He will. He'll pay for everything he has done to you and this kingdom."

"Promise?"

"I do," he said without hesitation. After another kiss on my forehead, he said, "Now, into the bed."

Sniffling, I let him help me stand up, and I climbed under the blankets fully clothed. I was too tired to bathe or change and figured

139

I would take care of it in the morning. Harrison nodded to let me know he heard my thoughts and I smiled at him.

"I missed you so much, Harrison," I yawned.

"I missed you, too, Rose. Love you. Good night."

"Love you, too. Good night."

When he turned to leave that time, I didn't stop him.

Chapter 16

Adele burst into the room the next morning as if there had been no time separating us, though I had no idea how early in the morning it was when she did. Not a word came from her mouth as she walked into the adjacent bathroom and started the bath. As if on a mission, she marched back into the room and stood next to the bed looking down at me, specifically my bald head.

Self-consciously, I rubbed my hand over the stubble that was already beginning to grow back. She shook her head swiftly, then met my eyes. Slowly, her face began to twist and her lower lip began to tremble. She brought her hands up to cover her face, but I had already seen. When her shoulders started shaking, I stood from the bed and held her.

"I am so sorry I left you," were the only words I understood as she wept and mumbled into my shoulder. I patted her back and made soft shushing sounds until she was finished. When she was done, she stepped back and rushed to the bathroom to shut off the water.

Stretching my arms over my head, I padded behind her. Leaning against the doorway, I watched her pour rose oil into my bath. "You know I do not blame you for any of this, right?"

She capped the rose oil bottle with tightly pressed lips and shook her head. Placing the bottle in the proper drawer, she said, "It does not matter whether you blame me or not. I cannot help but wonder if I had stayed, I could have helped you."

Gently, I took her hand in mine. She looked at me. "No, Adele. If you had stayed, Frank would have killed you for sure. There has been more death in Evergreen Palace in the last couple weeks than there has been since the founding of the kingdom. The things he did to people –" I thought of Earl and his lovely wife. "No. I am glad you escaped."

Adele nodded, though guilt still marred the expression on her face. "I am glad you are safe, Queen Miriam." She began to leave the bathroom.

"Adele?" I stopped her and she turned back to me. "Your friends, Christine and Bell. Are they safe?"

Tears filled her eyes. "Yes, Your Majesty. They are safe at the Petrichorian People's Base."

"Good. I am glad. You will stay here, though, when I go there, understood?"

Her eyes widened. "You cannot be serious, my Queen. We cannot have you so close to Frank. You are safest here in Sequoia."

"I must return to my home as soon as there is a plan to retake the kingdom. Petrichoria is the closest to home I can get right now."

"But Frank –"

"Is a monster and a beast, and I will see him imprisoned and tried before the Memorial Day of the Dazed if it is the last thing I do!" I was shouting near the end, but didn't realize it until I finished and a quiet filled the room. I was shaking in my fury, not that I was angry with Adele, but my growing animosity for Frank knew no bounds. "I am – sorry, Adele. I did not mean to shout."

Suddenly, Louis barged into the room. "Is everything alright in here?" he asked.

I gaped at him. "You are lucky I am still dressed, Louis."

He looked a little sheepish. "I just heard shouting and..." He shrugged.

Adele stepped aside to let me by so I could walk over to him. Quietly, I said, "Louis, we are safe here. We are underground and Frank does not know I am here." He nodded. "Now, what are you doing here? I thought you were going to contact and meet up with your family."

"They are all the way back in Petrichoria, my Queen of Hearts. I will return to them when you return there."

"Are you sure? I do not expect you to go with me."

"My duty is to see you safe. Where you go, I will go."

Touched by his loyalty, I said, "Very well. Thank you for your service. I am going to bathe now, though. So you can wait outside."

Louis bowed and went back to his post outside my door. I looked back to Adele, who was smiling. "I *am* sorry for yelling. You do not deserve that."

"I understand, Queen Miriam. You are righteously angry, and are passionate for your kingdom and your people. I am proud to be among them."

Not quite knowing what to say to that, I just nodded and went into the bathroom to get into the bath. It was warm and soothing on my aching legs. Though I could get around easily enough that morning, my legs had tired out and began to cramp already.

It was odd to not rush through the bath. I had nothing to fear where I was. Frank wouldn't be trying to make it back to catch me bathing or naked while changing, so there was no hurry. For the first time in, what seemed like, ages, I was able to completely relax and enjoy the soothing heat of the water.

After the water turned cold, I pulled myself up out of the tub, and wrapped a bath sheet around my body. One good thing about having no hair was that I didn't have to worry about drying it. I missed my hair anyway.

When I stepped out of the bathroom, Adele had laid out brown trousers and an emerald green sweater. In her hand, she held a satin ivory scarf and she was looking at it with an unusual amount of concentration.

"Everything alright?" I asked.

"Mmm-hmm," Adele responded, stroking her chin like an old man with a beard. "I must confess, Your Majesty, I am not experienced with scarf fashion."

I smiled. "I am sure whatever you do will look lovely."

"Ha. I appreciate your faith in my abilities. Even if it is undeserved."

I rolled my eyes. "It will be fine. No worries."

At that, she helped me get dressed and expertly applied some simple makeup. It took a while, but she did manage to wrap my head with the scarf beautifully. When she was done, I complimented her efforts and she cried like she did the first day we met; so happy that she was able to bring a smile to my face.

After hugging and crying a little more, Adele left me alone with my thoughts. As nice as it was to feel safe for once, I felt the same way Louis did, even if he wouldn't admit it. Though I had left no one personally behind, I felt an obligation to return as soon as possible to regain my kingdom. To set things right.

I bit at my thumb as I remembered Frank's violence in my recovery room. It was unlike him to be that way with me, but I supposed that was his point. If I somehow ended up back at the palace, things would be even more difficult than they already had been. Especially in light of my running away.

Gone would be the thin net of patience holding back Frank's desires and wrath. I shivered at the recollection of his will flowing through my veins, forcing me to do the unthinkable. I survived the last time I fought, but probably only barely. Pondering the surgery I had undergone, I stroked the silky scarf covering my bald head. Could I survive again? Would it kill me next time?

One thing was certain: I couldn't allow Harrison to come with me. I knew he would fight that, but I also knew that if the two of us ended up before Frank, Frank would make me kill him. I could never forgive myself for that. It would destroy me.

As if he could feel me thinking about him, which he probably could, Harrison knocked and entered at my greeting. He gave me an appraising look. "What dark thoughts are you having about me, Rose?"

"It's nothing," I lied. "Just not used to being safe yet."

"You know I can tell when you're lying to me."

"I know. But I also know that you trust me enough not to push it."

Harrison smirked. "Yeah. I do. I'll let it go, for now." He crossed the short distance between us and took my hands. Quietly, he said, "I didn't tell you this last night because, honestly, I wasn't sure if I was going to tell you this."

I quirked a brow at him. "What are you talking about?"

He sighed heavily. "I have a prisoner here you will definitely be interested in seeing."

"Who?"

Harrison pressed his lips together as if reconsidering whether to tell me. With a stiff nod, he finally spilled. "Prince Phineas of Britainnia."

"What? How have I not heard about this until now?"

"You just arrived last night."

"Well, yes. I meant, how didn't I hear that he had gone missing? I knew Frank kicked him out of the palace, at my insistence, but I thought he was in a safe house in the Willow province."

"He was. He was beginning to organize rebels in New America and decided to join them over there. A few faithful Arborians shot down his hover when he was heading east. This is headquarters, so he was brought here. He arrived shortly before you did yesterday."

I stared at him blankly for a few moments. Without Phin's betrayal, I was sure Frank probably still would have managed to overthrow the Crown, but it still stung. The memory of his brother and sister-in-law being shot and dying – his apology as he threw me to the floor and ran like the coward he was.

"I need to see him," I responded, just as quietly as he was speaking.

He looked down at our hands and squeezed as he nodded. "I figured. I came here to bring you to him. To get it over with."

"Yeah. Over with."

Without further comment, we went out the door and headed to the elevator. As we went to the bottom floor, I could feel him watching me, waiting for me to crack. Before, it would have annoyed me, but after everything I had been through, I was surprised, myself, that I hadn't broken like a porcelain doll thrown from the roof of Evergreen Palace. Because of that, I let him watch, choosing not to look back.

When the door opened, I took a deep, shuddering breath and allowed Harrison to pull me down the hall. Four doors down, we stopped and he opened the door with his handprint and eye scan. I stood in the open doorway, seeing one of the men responsible for the downfall of Arboria, lounging on a thin mattress like he was on vacation on the beaches of Atlantis.

146

Lazily, he turned his head to see who came in. It took a moment, but only a moment, for it to register who I was. His eyes and mouth widened with his shock, and I crossed my arms in front of me to stop myself from punching him in the face.

Harrison gently guided me in by the small of my back and the door slid shut behind us. Phin and I stared at each other for a bit before he broke the silence.

"Your hair," was what he said.

"My hair," I said coolly. "My *hair*?!" I said hotly. "You betray me at our wedding altar after agreeing to having both our families killed, all for your own personal gain, and the first thing you have to comment on is my *hair*?"

He winced each time I emphasized the word hair as if I was slapping him across the face. I wished I was. "Do you have any idea what is going on out there?" I asked, pointing at the door. With quiet vehemence, I continued. "He has killed *thousands* of my people. *Bodies* were clogging the street pipes and I had to send them out into the Petrichorian Sound with my own hands. Children were orphaned, and people were tortured and brutally murdered at his hands.

"Did you know he has the ability to force people to do his will with his words? He had me sit stone still when he tortured them. I had to watch and was powerless to stop him. You wonder what happened to my hair?" I tore off the scarf to reveal my peach fuzz and Phin's eyes began to water. "Frank tried to force himself on me with his ability and I fought him off. I fought harder than my brain could handle and I had a stroke; lost the use of my legs. Doctor Quincy had to shave my head to perform brain surgery so I could get the ability to use my legs back."

"I'm –"

"No," I snapped at his sobbing beginning of an apology. "Don't apologize. Nothing you say will mean a thing. Your tongue is blackened by your lies. After this moment, I never want to see you again." I turned my head to look at a dumb-struck Harrison. "He will be deported to Britainnia to face justice there. I wash my hands of him."

Harrison took the cue and opened the door for us to leave. "Miriam," Phin said, and I turned to face him.

Wisely, he stayed in his seat as he continued. "I know nothing I say can justify what I did. I wish I could say that Frank used his gift of compulsion on me, but he didn't. It was pure selfishness that drove me. I should have said no. I should have warned you. I should have been happy becoming your husband and King of Arboria. I should have done all those things and probably a hundred things more, but I didn't. There is nothing I can do about them, and the terrible things I have done will haunt me for the rest of my life, however short it may be. I am *sorry*."

I rewarded his heartfelt apology with a look empty of expression and left him with tears in his eyes.

Chapter 17

Harrison and I walked back to my room hand-in-hand. Back in the room, I tied the scarf back on my head, not nearly as nicely as Adele had done. Harrison watched me silently until I finished and faced him.

Was I an idiot for giving my heart away so quickly? Something deep inside told me Harrison was the one for me. I didn't know if it was God or my gift or gas, but I was sure about Harrison. I rushed over to him and relished in the feel of his strong arms around me. I began to weep uncontrollably as everything I lost came to mind. All my friends, my first love, ten years of my life, my family, and, finally, my kingdom. I didn't even have memories of my false life anymore.

Harrison kissed the top of my head. "It will all make sense in time."

I twitched and looked up at him with a feeling of déjà vu. "What did you say?"

"All of this? All this garbage that you're going through? God will work it out for good. You'll see."

"No," I murmured. He furrowed his brows. "No. What was it that you said? Word for word?"

He stopped and seemed to mentally rewind the short conversation. "It will all make sense in time?"

Suddenly, I began to hear that phrase in another voice, from another time, in another life.

It will all make sense in time.

Doctor Quincy had said that when I woke up, but before that, too.

One moment, I was being held in Harrison's arms, the next I was laying on my bed, and he was sitting on the bed next to me.

Looking at him, his head in his hands, I said, "How long this time?"

His head shot up. "Two hours. Did I stress you out by taking you for a visit with Phin?"

"No. You reminded me."

He cocked his head to the side. "Reminded you of what?"

"You reminded me of my false life." I was quiet, still processing everything that just happened. "It was like those words triggered it. I remember everything now. This life, that life." After a brief pause and a sigh, I added, "I have a new gift now, too. If I so desire, I can read a memory from someone's past if I'm touching someone's skin." I smirked. "I saw your memory of when you decided to become a part of the King's Test."

His cheeks flushed bright red and he cleared his throat. "That's, uh, quite a gift."

I chuckled and took his hand. "It feels more useful than the visions I get."

Harrison gently squeezed my hand. "Have you had any lately? Visions?"

Shaking my head, I said, "No, but even if I did have one, they haven't proven extremely useful, have they? There seems to be nothing I can do to prevent things from happening. I had visions about my friends in coffins and they all died. I had a dream of being in a glass coffin and I ended up in cryogenic freeze. I had a vision warning me of traitors in my midst, and there were. I had a vision of destruction on my wedding day and that happened, too."

Harrison shrugged. "Who knows why you have the visions. You may not have been able to stop any of those things from happening, but at least you had some warning, right? At least you knew *something* might happen. And now, this new part of your gift could be really helpful for you."

I looked at the ceiling as I thought about what he said. Maybe he was right. At least I knew about things before they happened. Perhaps the point wasn't to prevent what was going to happen, but prepare for it. The expectation of a perfect life was completely unreasonable.

Life had a way of kicking me down, hard, but that wasn't what ultimately mattered. What mattered was how I recovered from it. I didn't do so well the last time I was sucker-punched by the universe. I almost completely gave in to Frank. No more. It was time to fight for my people.

"It may help somehow, but I don't know how at the moment," I responded. Meeting his gaze, I said, "Harrison, I need to go back to Petrichoria."

"Are you insane?!" He shouted and stood. The more he spoke, the more upset he became. The more upset he became, the stronger his accent grew. "You can't go back there until things are settled, Rose! I promise you, Frank will not hesitate to constantly use his gift on you this time around if he gets his hands on you again. Not after your escape."

"I understand the risk," I replied calmly. "I don't intend on marching through the front doors of Evergreen Palace. I plan on

151

going to the People's Base there. We can make our plans via holocomm while I'm there."

Harrison's eyes darkened as it dawned on him what I meant. "You think I'm not coming."

"No. I *know* you're not coming."

"You honestly think I would let you go back without me? Alone?"

"No. I won't be alone. Louis needs to get back to Petrichoria, too. His family is there. We'll go together."

Harrison sat back down on the bed and caged me in by placing both arms on either side of my hips on the bed. Nearly touching noses, he said quietly, but still with a thick accent, "Let's get something straight, my love. I will not send you into danger alone. If you want to go to Petrichoria, fine. But I'm coming with you. There will be no further discussion about it. Are we clear?"

His tone allowed no argument. At that moment I figured out I wouldn't be getting my way. I knew he would put up a fight, but I had no idea I wouldn't win it.

"Are we clear?" Harrison repeated.

"As crystal." I confirmed.

With a stiff nod, he stood up and went to the door. "I'll see you this evening for the feast. I'll be back by 5:00 to get you." He paused in the doorway and turned around. "I love you, Rose. I walked away from you once, but I will never do that again."

"Okay," I replied eloquently, hardly believing how insistent he was being.

I spent the next couple of hours tossing and turning, trying to rest before the feast, but unable to because my mind wouldn't shut off.

Will someone else betray me? Will Frank find me here? What will he do to me if he finds me? How am I going to take the Crown from him? How will he be punished? Do I have the guts to put him to death? Is that even what I want? Will my people have it any other way? What about all the other traitors?

On and on my brain went. Sleep I desperately needed, because of my brain download, I was sure, eluded me. When I was about to give up, Adele came in whistling. Seeing me in bed, she stopped in her tracks. "Are you feeling alright, Miriam?"

"Just tired," I replied, still staring at the ceiling. "The memories from my false life came back to me this morning and I have not been able to rest since then, though I have felt the need for it. Do we have anything for headaches in here?"

"Well, that is great! Not the restlessness or sleeplessness or headache part, but your memory. That is fantastic. I will see if we have anything for your headache in the bathroom." Adele hustled off, and I heard drawers opening and closing in the other room. "Here we go," she said as she approached the bed, holding out a pill and a glass of water.

I sat up and took the proffered pill, praying silently that it would work quickly. "Thank you."

"You are welcome. Now." She clapped her hands once loudly, shocking me into a jolt. "Tonight's feast will have some guests you may not be expecting. Some allies of ours are already here, and we are expecting General Patrick Maddon of Southland and a troop of his forces to arrive in time for it."

That surprised me and I said so. "Southland is coming?"

Adele playfully slapped my arm. "Of course they are, Your Majesty. Queen Natalie gave an ultimatum to Frank. She is following through on it."

"Wow." I undressed silently, thinking about the number of people we would have fighting Frank. "What other allies do we have?"

"Well," Adele began, bringing my green gown over my head, then leading me over to the vanity to begin on my makeup. Draping a cloth around my shoulders so we didn't mess up the dress, she said, "There is Atlantis. Prince Liam came with them." I blushed as I remembered my rude dismissal of him at the King's Test. I was frightened and believed him not human, though now I knew he was. "Prince Leonardo from Swiss-France brought a legion. Generals from New California and New America have brought support as well, though I cannot remember their names."

I blanched. "How have all of these people come into our country unnoticed by Frank and his people?"

"Ah. I am not sure about the technical details, my Queen of Hearts, but from what I understand, Lucas was able to get some kind of codes that allowed us to block the satellites from seeing our part of the coastline. Atlantis brought them in their submarines."

"All of them?"

"Yes, all of them."

I stayed quiet as she applied my lip color, then said, "I cannot believe how much Prince Liam has helped. Why has he helped so much?"

"He has not given any specific reason, but I would imagine he would like to keep good relations with Arboria in the future and he figures this is a way to ensure that."

"And Prince Leonardo is here?"

"Yes, Your Majesty."

I closed my eyes. "I do not know how I will face him. I feel partially responsible for Domonique's death. I wish there was a way I could have stopped it."

She had been done with my makeup for a minute, but at my words, she spun my chair and sank to her knees in front of me. Grabbing my hands fiercely, and with a ferocious look in her eyes, she admonished me. "Don't you say that, Miriam." I knew she meant business because she abandoned grammar etiquette, which she never did.

"Her death is *not* your fault. Neither was the death of King George or your parents or Duke Peter or anyone else for that matter. You were used and manipulated by a man who was supposed to become your husband, then abused by Frank. I haven't spoken to a single soul that blames you."

Tears were welling up in my eyes. I had no concern for my makeup because none of it would run. "All that death, Adele. Thousands of lives. I married that brute to prevent death and it happened anyway. How is that not my fault?"

"Perhaps it would have been worse if there were bombs going off. Perhaps we would be dealing with the deaths of those in the explosions and those who died from the fighting. Perhaps he would have won anyway. Or maybe there were never any bombs and it was all a bluff. I don't know and neither do you. But, my Queen of Hearts, you cannot continue to dwell on this. If you must, let it inspire you toward victory against Frank."

A final tear fell down my cheek as I sat there, mouth agape, at Adele. Where did that come from?

"Thank you, Adele," I said.

Standing and beginning to wrap the scarf on my head, she simply replied, "Anytime." Nothing more was said as she intricately wrapped my head with the scarf and topped it off with my mother's crown. Stroking the gems that always seemed so delicate to me, I began to cry again.

This wasn't the way it was meant to be. It was always a possibility that Father and Mother would die before I took over, but they were supposed to outlive my coronation as Queen. Father was supposed to pass the crown to me.

I had pictured the day so many times growing up. Father and Mother would walk me down the aisle of the church. When they left me at the altar, the priest would perform the ceremony with me looking out at my fellow Arborians. Father and Mother would be standing together, Mother with tears in her eyes. Stephan and Ella would be there, of course. Later on in my life, Peter became a part of the vision, standing with me, becoming King while I became Queen.

That's not at all how it actually happened. Instead, my parents had been brutally murdered, my fiancé had betrayed me, and my husband was an egomaniac. Our acceptance as King and Queen was done without my being present by a group of Nobles personally selected by Frank and his father. I was Queen and I hadn't celebrated at all because it was tainted.

"Do you think she is proud of me?" I said almost absentmindedly.

"Absolutely," Adele said without hesitation, then cleared her throat. "Prince Harrison will be here soon. I will go so you can collect yourself. For what it is worth, Your Majesty, *I* am proud to call you my Queen."

She left without waiting for a response and I just stood and stared at the woman in the mirror. I almost wished I looked like Mother so I might catch a glimpse of her in my own reflection, but my features had always been those of Father.

With the way the scarf draped along my shoulders and neck, no one would be able to notice my missing hair. Though, that didn't really matter. Everyone knew about it anyway. I was so deep in my pity pool that I barely heard the knock at the door.

Solemnly, I went to the door and opened it for Harrison. I didn't meet his gaze; I couldn't even look at him. There he was, ready to celebrate, and I had managed to put myself in a funk. He tipped my chin up so I was looking at him.

"I think you sometimes forget that I can read your mind," he said gently.

"Right."

"You've been thinking on some pretty terrible things all afternoon, darlin'. I didn't come to you because I felt you needed some time. Besides, Adele was with you."

"Yeah."

Harrison cupped my face in his big hands. "It. Is. Not. Your. Fault."

Tears formed in my eyes. He continued. "It's not. There is nothing you could do beyond what you've done. You kept Frank leashed for as long as you could." With his thumb, he gently stroked my slightly purple cheek from where Frank struck me. "I mean, he actually struck you. No one blames you for running."

"It wasn't the first time," I muttered. "There was a difference, though. The first time, he felt bad about it. This time, he just about promised more if I didn't cooperate." Harrison's expression turned into a scowl. "I feel – I don't deserve to be Queen of these people, Harrison. I couldn't give myself to him, no matter what he said he would give me. I –"

"Stop. Stop, Rose." His look said it all. *I* wasn't the mind-reader and I could tell what he was thinking. He wanted to kill Frank. He didn't blame me and he didn't think anyone else would either.

"What have I done, Harrison?" Whispering now, I was venting everything out on him. A small part of me felt bad, considering we were on our way to a celebration, but I couldn't hold it in anymore. "I was the only thing holding him back. Now, I'm afraid he will do whatever it takes to get me back."

Harrison gently led me back into the room, then stepped away, running a hand through his perfectly coiffed hair – it wasn't perfectly coiffed anymore. Hands akimbo, he said, "I just don't get it, Rose."

"Don't get what?"

"His obsession with you. I mean, don't get me wrong, darlin'. You're my everything. It's why I'm here, but him? His whole goal has been to become King. He's *there*. He has what he wants. His theory that having you by his side would smooth things over with the people didn't go his way, so you'd think he would just, I don't know, leave you be or kill you or imprison you or something besides trying to get you into his bed."

Looking at my feet, I said, "He wants me to have his children. He wants *our* children to be his heirs to the Crown."

"But *why*? Why you? With his numbers, there has to be someone willing to be his Queen. Someone he doesn't have to convince or use his gift on."

I walked over to him and smoothed out his hair as best I could. "Look, Harrison. He's insane. That's why you can't figure him out. It is impossible. I gave up trying to figure him out a long time ago. One thing is for certain, though. I won't let my people suffer for me. I have to take back the Crown as soon as possible."

Harrison rubbed my arms with his hands before pulling me into an embrace and resting his cheek on the top of my head. "I know, I know," he murmured, then sighed. Pulling back with a smile, he added, "For now, try to set it aside and celebrate tonight. Just before your arrival, our allies arrived and will be joining us tonight."

I placed my face in my hands with a groan and an echo of his sigh. "I think I can do that. Adele filled me in on our guests, though she didn't know the names of all the generals. She knew General Maddon, but not the generals from New California or New America."

"General Lee of New California and General Cook from New America."

"Thanks," I mumbled and flushed a bit. "I – I feel a little embarrassed to see Liam again."

Harrison raised an eyebrow. "Do I want to know?"

I scratched the back of my neck and stepped back. "You have to remember that *I* didn't remember *anything* from this life during the very, very brief time I knew him." I chuckled nervously, remembering how I gently stroked his neck, trying to follow his custom, and discovering his – gills. Noticing his unease and struggle to stay out of my head, I cleared my throat. "And the only time I really spoke with him was – was –"

"Was during the first round of the King's Test. The kissing round. Again, I ask, do I really want to know?"

"Probably not," I said as his self-control slipped a little too soon and caught my brain replaying the memory. When his eyes widened, I couldn't stop it and he couldn't stop watching.

We just had a misunderstanding. Just what I needed, to culturally offend someone visiting Arboria for the first time. Someone competing to become the next King. Way to blow it, Miriam. As if there aren't enough things to worry about already.

He tilts my chin and I tense up for the first kiss. Another one. I'm surprised that he doesn't kiss my lips, but trails and swirls his tongue along my neck, below my ear. I try to pull away, but he pulls me closer, apparently determined to finish – whatever this is.

When my body is pressed closely to his, he kisses me soundly on the lips, gently brushing the spot on my neck where his tongue just was with his fingers. Something feels wrong – more wrong than having so many first kisses. Something wrong with this kiss.

Hoping to relax him into ending the kiss, I follow what I assume is some kind of cultural thing and stroke his neck, too. He groans into my mouth and deepens the kiss, rather than end it, and that's when I feel the pulsing and opening of three slits.

Harrison was finally able to pull out of the memory at that point. What prevented him from pulling out in the first place? Morbid curiosity? Jealousy? I had no idea, but his reaction was completely unexpected. His eyes were still wide, but not as wide as the giant smile that flew up onto his face. Boyish mirth took over his whole demeanor as he began to laugh uncontrollably.

"It's not funny, Harrison!" I said maturely with a stomp of my foot, making him laugh harder.

"You – you – you didn't know! You didn't know!" Harrison continued his laughing.

"How was I to know? No one told me!"

"Holy tornados! It's too much." He was, then, wiping tears from his eyes from laughing too hard.

"Okay," I said, smirking. "Maybe it *is* a little funny, but it's also embarrassing. Can you see now how I don't know how I'll face him?"

"Wait," Harrison took a deep breath to calm himself down. "So, *that's* why Liam went home? His gills?"

"It totally freaked me out! Everyone tried assuring me that he was still human, but I just couldn't get past it. Back in the twenty-first century, Atlantis was a myth. If anyone actually believed it existed, they assumed it was in ruins, its people dead for thousands of years. The idea of Atlantis fascinated me. I was excited to meet Liam, but –"

"But life was already one huge ball of surprises and challenges, and you couldn't handle another one. I get it. I'm sure, now knowing what you were going through, he gets it, too."

I blanched. "What do you mean 'now knowing what I was going through?' No one is supposed to know about my memory loss."

"Ah. Yeah. About that – I probably should have told you. It wasn't me. I don't rightly know who it was, but someone let that snake out from under the rock and it spread … Everyone knows. Everyone."

"What?!"

"Their reaction wasn't what you thought it would be," he said quickly. "You thought they would refuse you, turn against you, but it was the opposite, Rose. When they discovered your problem, they rallied even more to your name. When they learned that the problem was in the past and your memory returned, they rejoiced.

"Your people love you. Unconditionally." He paused at his statement. "Although, had you accepted Frank and his cruelty with open arms, and made the deaths of your people worthless, they may have stopped."

I smacked his arm playfully, then sobered up. "So, there's nothing more to hide."

"There is that, too."

It was an incredible feeling. Even with everything going on around me, I felt as if a huge load was lifted. I didn't have to lie to anyone anymore. At least that part of my problem was done and over with.

"Okay. I can do this," I assured myself while pretending to assure Harrison.

"Of course you can, darlin'."

I smirked. "I like that."

"What?"

"'Darlin'.' Your accent, in general." I wrapped my arms around his waist. "And I get to hear it for the rest of my life."

"Indeed, you do. Now. We're very late. We need to go."

I shrugged. "I'm the Queen of Hearts. I can be late to my own party if I want."

Chapter 18

I'm not sure what I was expecting, but a hanger full of random sizes and shapes of tables and people was not it. How this was all set up, I had no idea. Who had time to set all that up and make all that food? How did word already get out to all these people?

It wasn't fancy. There were no chandeliers hanging from the tall ceiling. The concrete floor didn't shine and wasn't engraved. Like the ballrooms at Evergreen Palace. The people, my people and allies, weren't dressed in finery, as I was, but in their uniforms. Well, that wasn't entirely true. Both Prince Liam and Prince Leonardo were dressed finely, as well.

We paused in the doorway as everyone stood and began to applaud. There were whoops and hollers and random shouts of "Long live the Queen of Hearts" and "We love you, Queen Miriam!" Smiles were on every face and people reached out to touch my arm as I walked past to get to the table at the front where the Princes and Generals were standing and clapping before their seats.

It was overwhelming. It was stressful. It was wonderful. I had never felt so much love and trust from any group of people in my entire life. Being in crowds wasn't a new thing for me; I had been a Princess my whole life, after all. I always knew my people had a fondness for me, but this was different.

Perhaps learning my whole story gave them some new insight into who I was. Perhaps my being kidnapped and having the kingdom stolen straight out of my hands frightened everyone, and they were just relieved to see me again. Perhaps all the sacrifices I had made were not in vain and the people were responding to them.

I wasn't sure what inspired such a reaction from so many people, but there it was. Harrison and I reached the table at the end of the room and the applause died down. While the two of us remained standing, everyone else took a seat. I glanced at the men sitting at the table near me. The Generals were smiling, as were the Princes, though Leon's face seemed a bit forced, which didn't surprise me. Just as I had experienced loss, he had, too. I nodded to him in understanding and he nodded back.

When the room was quiet, I squeezed Harrison's hand and sent a silent signal to him that he could take a seat, even though my heart was beating so fast I was sure it was going to burst out of my chest. The room full of people looked at me expectantly, the way they used to look at Father and Mother before they spoke. Could I measure up?

"People of Arboria, friends, and allies," I began, my voice naturally amplified in the large hanger. "I am truly humbled and blessed by the outpouring of your love and trust this day.

"These past few weeks have been trying for all of us. We have lost our friends. We have lost our family. We have lost our kingdom. A false King has taken over and changed the face of Arboria. Our name? Gone. Our colors? Changed. The Nobles? Different. Council Chambers? Now a Throne Room.

"Yes. He has made changes to even the fundamental structure of our government. However, he hasn't – he won't change us. He won't change you. I am touched and encouraged by your loyalty and willingness to fight. Together, we will remove Frank from power. Together, we will take back the kingdom of Arboria."

Though I didn't feel like I had said anything particularly extraordinary, the people stood to their feet and began applauding again. Some were elbowing each other and laughing. Others were weeping, whether from joy or sadness from our losses, I didn't know. Then, a few people at a time, each person sank into a bow of respect. Even the allies, who weren't even my citizens, bowed.

Finally, Harrison stood and took my hand again. Being his articulate, princely self, he announced, "Thanks for the fine words, my love. Let's feast and celebrate the return of our Queen of Hearts!"

Grateful for the change in atmosphere, I took my seat as everyone stood straight and took theirs. Amiable chatting began around the room as the food got passed around and plates were loaded. It was like a giant family feast.

I was so enthralled with watching everyone, I had no idea conversations were being had at the table, and Harrison was putting an ungodly amount of food on my plate until I looked at it. I looked up at him and he wasn't even watching what he was doing; he was talking with Prince Liam about something that had all the men at the table chuckling or grinning with glee. I figured I should probably start paying attention.

"– So, you see, no one warned her! While all of us have had decades to get to know the Atlantean people, she still believed Atlantis was little more than a myth. And there she was making out with a man with gills!"

Everyone laughed, including Prince Liam, and I flushed bright red. I shot Harrison a glare because he was sharing such a personal story, but all he did was wink at me and set down the potatoes. I felt like a teenager whose mother was showing naked baby pictures to all her friends.

Prince Liam slapped Harrison on the back with a hand as he laughed heartily. He looked at me with mirth and asked, "Is this true, Queen Miriam? Had I known about your memory problem, I surely would have filled you in. It is not like they are a secret."

I cleared my throat and promised Harrison vengeance in my head. He choked on a drink he was taking and grinned maniacally. "Yes. I am afraid it is true, Prince Liam. Of course, now, I feel terribly embarrassed by it all. I hope my behavior has not offended you or your people too badly."

He sobered immediately and grabbed my hand, even though he sat two people away from me. Meeting my gaze, he said, "Queen Miriam, if I was offended, do you think I would be here now with my Navy?"

"Yes," I said without hesitation. "I think you would because I know more about you now. Adele, my assistant, told me about how you have been bringing our allies from all over the continent here in your submarines. You have seen my people's plight and have done everything in your power to help us. I would like you to know how much I appreciate your assistance, despite my seemingly rude reaction those weeks ago."

Prince Liam released my hand and sat back. "I will admit, I was confused by being let go so early in the King's Test, but not offended. Atlantis will always be there for Arboria, Queen Miriam. You have my word on that."

"Thank you." I looked at the rest of the table. Everyone else was well on their way to being finished with their food, while my mountain of meat, potatoes, and vegetables was still untouched. "Thank you. All of you. In the past, Arboria has been quite isolated from the world. If not for this most recent King's Test and the Queen of Southland's request of her allies, I am not sure what we would be doing right now. Certainly not celebrating anything."

"If I may, Your Majesty," an unfamiliar male voice said. I looked over to who I assumed was the General of New America's Army, based on his green dress uniform with a red, white, and blue flag pinned along with his medals. "We would have come to your aid even if the Queen of Southland had not given her ultimatum to Frank Miller.

166

"While your people have remained isolated in the past, we know that you are a peaceful people. Many times in history, megalomaniacs have stomped on such people, destroying what was built and creating chaos where there was once order. The number of lives lost on the night of Frank Miller's takeover," General Cook shook his head. "We could not stand by and watch what he was doing. Queen Natalie simply gave us the push we needed to move forward."

General Lee nodded. "I agree. What has been done here is atrocious. We are honored to help you in your time of need."

"Alright! Let's clear these tables to allow for some dancing," announced Lucas and his band, who were set up on the side of the room. Apparently, everyone was done eating. I glanced down at my untouched plate again, not even hungry for it. I knew someone had put a lot of work into it, but I couldn't touch it.

Don't feel bad, darlin'. Everyone understands.

Harrison's reassuring words floated through my mind as our plates were cleared. I gave the gentleman clearing mine a sheepish look and he simply smiled in return, affirming Harrison's message to me.

At an amazing pace, tables and chairs were folded and put away. People stood on the sides of the room, looking at the band with delightful anticipation. Lucas gave everyone that siren's smile and said, "We are the Band of Roses. In honor of our Queen of Hearts' arrival, we would like to open this evening's dancing with The Rose. Your Majesty, please do us the honor of starting our night off right."

I never knew his band's real name and felt oddly honored by the reference to my nickname. Without hesitancy, I grabbed Harrison's hand and pulled him out onto the dancefloor. Hoots and whistles surrounded us, and I was glad for the informality of the evening.

The Band of Roses played an eerie version of The Rose in a minor key. Out of all the balls and festivities I had opened a dance with the familiar song, it had to be my favorite. If nothing else, it was the most unique rendition I had ever heard.

Harrison held me close and his blue, blue eyes met mine. It felt so nice to be back in his arms again. Our relationship happened so fast. I remembered all those cheesy romance novels I had ever read. All those times I scoffed at the main character for falling in love within the first few days of knowing someone. "That's impossible," I would mutter to myself. "No one falls in love that quickly."

However, that's exactly how it had happened with Harrison. Ever since that first time I saw him from the stairs of the Core. All tall and blond. A Texan god, I think was how I referred to him when talking to Mother. I smiled at the memory and I could see Harrison was amused by my thought.

Just what you need for your low self-esteem, I thought to him. His grin grew bigger.

The night wore on and I danced with so many different people. It reminded me of the way the United States used to be. A melting pot of diversity. I danced with Arborians and Atlanteans, Californians and Americans, Princes and soldiers. It was an incredible night that I never wanted to end. For just a few hours, there was no Frank Miller. No one was dead. For just a few hours, everything was right in the world.

On the way back to my room, Harrison swung our linked hands like we were small children walking together through the playground. I was smiling. I couldn't remember the last time I had smiled. Before Frank invaded, that was for sure. But all things must come to an end.

When we entered my room, I turned to Harrison to speak, but he pressed his index finger against my lips, successfully hindering any words from coming out. "Oh, no. Not tonight, Rose."

"But –" I muffled against his finger.

"No. Not tonight. I know you want to plan. I know you want to get to Petrichoria and stop Frank. I know. It will happen, but tonight, let's just be together." His hand lowered and wrapped around my waist so he could pull me to him.

"Together?" I wanted to be with him, but not until we were married. I had made the promise before God and my parents long ago to wait until my wedding night to make love. While I loved Harrison, I had no intention of breaking that vow then.

"Not like that, darlin'."

I relaxed, only then even realizing I tensed up. "I just want to be with you a little longer, until you fall asleep. Then, I'll leave. Last night, when I left you all sad and dejected – Well, I just didn't do so well. I hated leaving you like that."

"Okay. We can do that. I'll go put on my night clothes and be right back." I got up on my tip toes and pecked him on the cheek. He gave a sigh of relief and released me to go change.

After popping by my dresser to get a nightgown, I went into the bathroom and hopped into the shower. Tilting my head back, I let the steaming water run down my fuzzy head and down my back, cleansing my body and soul. I breathed the steam in through my nose and released the hot air through my mouth. I missed the feel of my long hair down my back. In time, I knew, it would grow back.

Suddenly, there was a knock at the bathroom door. Leaving the water running, I stepped out and wrapped a towel around myself. I cracked the door open and peeked out at Harrison, who was holding a small bottle of something in his hand.

"What's that?" I asked him.

"A gift from Prince Leonardo," he said with a smirk, which I thought was an odd reaction. Most men would feel jealous or intimidated by another man giving gifts to his woman. Then again,

Harrison knew my mind and was probably confident that there was really no competition as far as I was concerned.

He handed me the gold-toned bottle. It read "Champoing de Repousse des Cheveux." I knew I should have learned French. "You didn't answer my question."

"You don't know French?"

"You know I don't, mind-reader."

He laughed. "You really don't know what this is? The Swiss-French have developed a serum that accelerates hair growth. It's popular among their actors and actresses who frequently have to cut or shave their hair for a role. Leon heard about what happened and had some sent up from New California."

I shot my gaze from the bottle to him. "Are you serious? Don't tease me about this."

"I'm serious. I can't believe you've never heard of this stuff. One time, my sister fell out of a tree and had to get stitches down the side of her head. They shaved her whole head so her hair would grow back evenly, applied this stuff, and it was past her shoulders the next morning."

"How have I never heard of this?"

Harrison shrugged. "That's what happens, I guess, when you're asleep for ten years."

"But, why didn't anyone tell me about this? Why didn't Frank tell me about this?"

"Because Frank is a manipulative jerk. Everyone else probably just assumed you knew about it. I think we forget sometimes that you missed ten years. Sorry, darlin'." Harrison frowned. "You mean, ever since they shaved your head, you thought you were going to have to wait for your hair to grow back?"

I nodded numbly. "It was such a silly thing to be concerned about. I should have just been happy to have my legs back."

"It's not silly, darlin'. Well, I guess it *is* a little silly, considering everything else going on." I glared at him and he laughed. "Oh, honey. I should have known you were thinking about that. There's no good reason I didn't besides I wasn't paying close enough attention. Your hair will be back to its full length after a couple days of applying this at night."

My eyes filled with tears. "Thank you, Harrison. Thank Leon for me, too." I closed the door and stepped back in the shower, holding the bottle close to my chest like it was the Holy Grail. I squeezed some of the viscous liquid into the palm of my hand and it tingled. After massaging it into my scalp and rinsing, being careful not to get it anywhere I didn't want growing a ton of hair, I washed the rest of my body, dried off, and got into my green nightgown.

By the time I walked out of the bathroom, I was exhausted. So was Harrison, by the looks of it. He was much too long for the couch he was sprawled across; his legs were dangling over the arm on one side. He looked over to me from staring at something seemingly interesting on the ceiling.

"I'm ready," I said.

"You look it, darlin'."

He got up and followed me over to my bed. I climbed under the blankets and he tucked the blankets into my sides. I felt cocooned, safe. Then, he sat on the side of the bed and stared at me. I laughed nervously.

"I don't know that I can fall asleep with you staring at me."

"Try," he said quietly, then stroked my cheek with a finger. Sure enough, the soft motion soothed me and my eyes grew heavy.

"I'll have hair tomorrow," I mumbled sleepily.

Harrison chuckled. "Yeah, you will."

The last thing I remembered before falling asleep was the feel of Harrison's lips brushing over mine in a good night kiss.

Chapter 19

I sit in my tree house, my safe house, twirling my hair through my fingers and listening to rain hit the roof. It's the length I imagine it will be when I wake up in the morning. I am going to do something either brave or stupid or both. Part of me thinks I shouldn't do it. The other part is done being afraid.

I stand up and call him into my presence. He appears, looking confused. "What?" He looks around the tiny room. He's never been in here, so he probably has no idea where he is. He also doesn't know about this particular talent of mine. "Where is this?"

"This is my childhood treehouse," I respond and walk over to the wall, tracing the "S & R" that Stephan and I carved into it so many years ago.

"Alright. My imagination is a little weird tonight," he mutters to himself. "Your hair is back. Glad to see it."

I look at him coolly. "This isn't your imagination. It's mine. I brought you here."

His face blanches. "No way."

Without reluctance, I walk over and pinch his bicep hard. "Ouch!" he yells. "What did you do that for?"

"You don't feel pain in normal dreams, Frank. You're really here."

He frowns, rubbing his arm. "Still makes no sense. You're away from me. Why would you bring me here? Wait. Were you communicating with the rebels that whole time? Is that how you escaped?"

"Not the whole time. Not that I didn't try. Naturally, I didn't know who was and was not in the resistance, so I couldn't contact just anyone. I tried to contact Harrison for weeks, but couldn't because we were never sleeping at the same time. I was finally able to and we arranged my escape from the hospital."

Frank walks over to me. "I'm going to find you, Rose."

"Good luck with that."

"Why did you bring me here?"

"I was sitting in here, thinking about how much safer the world will be once I am Queen of Arboria again."

"So you're coming back to me?" Frank has that ridiculous look of hope he always gets when he thinks I'm surrendering to him.

"Never." His look deflates, like I kicked his puppy. "I am going to take back my kingdom, Frank. I'm going to take it back, divorce you, and give the King's crown to Harrison. Then, I'm going to burn the thrones you had made in the city center as a symbol of the fall of your short tyranny."

Frank slaps me, but hurts his hand instead of me. In my dreams, I'm invincible. I am stone. Nothing and no one can hurt me.

"You may have the power here, Rose, but out there, I am King."

"Not for much longer."

With a single thought, I send him away back to whatever fantasy he was experiencing before I brought him to me. He'll be afraid now, or at least I hope he will be. Now, I plan. I'm going to remind him who I am and he's going to learn what happens to those who go against those I love.

When I wake up, Harrison is gone, as he promised. I thought about my dream and what I did. Was it stupid? Maybe. Did I feel better after doing it? Absolutely.

I stood up and stretched, and absently ran my fingers through my hair that fell down to my upper back, then stopped. I pulled the dark tresses around to my face and stared at them for a moment, then pressed them against my cheek and sobbed. My hair was back. No matter what anyone else said, I knew it was a silly thing to care about at a time like that, when my kingdom was out of my hands, and a monster sat on a throne literally of his own design and making.

My joy was short-lived, however, when Harrison came bursting into the room without knocking, fear etched on his face. "I don't know how it happened," was all he said.

"What's going on?" I demanded.

"Frank's army is here at our door, Rose."

"What?"

"It was me," a soft voice said behind Harrison. I looked around him and saw the last person I would ever expect to betray me.

"No. Not you."

"Yes, my Queen. Frank says if you come out alone, in peace, he will leave this place untouched. He also wanted me to remind you that those bombs from your wedding day are still placed strategically around the kingdom. He apparently left them, just in case," Louis said.

I strode over to him and slapped him across the face. "Et tu Louis?"

"You don't understand —" he pleaded. Harrison stood by with his hand over his mouth and a look of shock on his face.

"Frank has his family," Harrison said.

"Why didn't you say something?" I asked Louis.

"Frank said he would hurt them if you had warning," Louis begged. "Please. I didn't know how he would find out or how what he would do, but I couldn't let him hurt my family."

I shot a look at Harrison, then looked back to Louis and I knew it was true. Of anyone in the world, aside from Harrison, Louis was the one I trusted the most. Things had to be dire for him to do something like this. I knew the horrible decisions I had made myself under duress from Frank. He was a force to be reckoned with.

It was all my fault. It was because of the dream. If I had left everything alone, perhaps everything would be alright now. I pressed my lips together into a straight line.

"When?"

"When we arrived, Lucas helped me contact my family at the Petrichorian People's Base. He left me alone to comm them. The General there said my wife and daughter had gone up for air, not an unusual thing, but strayed too far and were caught. Frank broadcast a message only in Petrichoria when he discovered who they were related to. He said if I came forward and told him where you were, he would release them and let us live.

"I contacted Evergreen Palace and gave them our coordinates. I am sorry, my Queen of Hearts. I know I have committed treason, but I could not let my family die."

I simply nodded. "How long do we have, Louis?"

"Frank contacted me a few minutes ago. You have an hour to go up to him."

Turning to Frank, I asked, "How far away are we from the New California border?"

"Too long to make several trips with the Atlantean submarines," he replied, knowing my thoughts. "We can get probably half of the people here gone with those subs. The rest –"

"Will have to depend on Frank's word," I finished for him when he didn't finish the phrase. "Rotting roots!" I punched a hole in the wall and my fist began to bleed. I was sure I broke something. Louis' eyes widened in fear and Harrison lunged forward to take my fractured hand into his.

"Harrison, I need you to call an emergency meeting with the Princes and Generals. Make arrangements for the evacuation of as many of our troops as possible. Take the Generals' advisement under consideration when you decide who will go and who will stay. Louis, please grab the first aid kit from my bathroom."

The two men eyed each other. Harrison looked at Louis with anger and fury, but Louis just looked haggard and defeated. I touched Harrison with my unhurt hand. "Harrison, tell me honestly that you wouldn't have done the same if it was me and our child."

Harrison's expression softened and he gently released my hand. "I honestly don't know what I would have done in your position, Louis. All I know is that you've brought Hell down on us. I'm not sure there is forgiveness from me here." He swallowed hard as he turned back to me. "I know you'll give yourself up, Rose. I know it and I hate it, but I understand it." He wrapped me in his big arms and kissed me like he would never see me again, then left without another word.

Silently, Louis went to the bathroom and grabbed the first aid kit. After I sat down, he picked up my hand and used the cut weaver to stop the bleeding. Because I clearly didn't have clean breaks, it was difficult to wrap, but he managed.

"Can you find Adele for me, Louis? I would like to at least be dressed when I surrender myself again."

"Of course, Your Majesty."

177

Somehow, I ended up standing in front of my closet, running my fingers over the beautiful greens I would be leaving behind. I couldn't remember walking over there. I selected an emerald green sweater and ivory trousers with chocolate brown boots and set them on the edge of the bed. Because of my temper, I would be unable to dress myself.

Adele walked in to find me staring at the clothes. She placed a hand on my shoulder and I looked up at her. Tears were streaming down her cheeks. Abandoning the formality she loved, she said, "I'm so sorry this is happening to you again."

Blankly, I said, "I don't know if I can stop him this time." Stop him from what went unsaid. From continuing his dictatorship. From torturing and murdering people in his Throne Room of blood. From taking my virginity and forcing me to bear his children. He was right in the dream. I was powerless outside my dream world.

It took a half hour for her to clean me up, help me into my clothing, and do my hair and makeup. I stepped out into the hallway and found Louis waiting patiently. Harrison was with him.

"No," I said, not needing to be a mind-reader to know why Harrison was there.

"Yes," Harrison said.

"Harrison, if Frank sees you with me, he will make me kill you. He has told me that is what he will do. I won't be able to live with myself. You are too important to me and this movement. You must go with the submarines." To further make my point, I ran through the memory of Frank threatening me, knowing Harrison was in my mind.

I saw his Adam's apple bob with his swallowing. He hated that I was right. In my defense, I hated that I was right, too. He took me up in his arms and kissed me again, not caring that Adele and Louis were standing right there. I wasn't sure how long we stood there like that, but it wasn't long enough. Before too long, he had to go so he could make the submarine on time. After one more wistful look, he took Adele's hand and dragged her down the hallway away from me. She fought him. She wanted to come with me, but Harrison knew I wanted her to go to safety, too.

When they were gone, without looking at him, I said, "Alright. Let's go, Louis."

Letting him lead the way, I walked with stooped shoulders and my hand to my temple, massaging away a forming headache. I said I wanted to go back to Petrichoria and there I was – going back. Not exactly what I meant when I said it.

I thought of the celebration the night before. All the feasting, dancing and singing. All for naught. Now that I was thinking about it, I realized that Louis hadn't been there the night before. It made sense. At least I knew it wasn't my stupidity that brought Frank down on our heads. Louis had betrayed me before I brought Frank into my dream.

We reached the end of the hall and climbed into the waiting elevator. Awkwardly, we took it to the top. When we hit the top floor, I jabbed my finger onto the button to keep the door closed and held it there. Louis did nothing but patiently wait for me to release the button. He wouldn't use force on me. I knew it. He knew it. I could have made my escape on a submarine and sentenced half the people in the Base, and Louis and his family, to death.

But that wasn't the person I was. I was the true Queen of these people. That's why they loved me. That's why they reached out to touch me as I passed them last night. That's why they danced with me. That's why they would always be loyal to me.

I was Queen and my people would always come first.

Part III

Chapter 20

Finally, I released the button and the door opened. I thought it would lead straight outside, but, much to my chagrin, there was a flight of stairs with a hatch door I would need to open. I just wanted it to be over with.

I sighed and led Louis up the stairs. Trying the hatch myself, I discovered I wasn't strong enough to open it, especially with my mashed-up hand. Just great. I needed another reminder about how powerless I was. Louis gently pushed me aside and opened the hatch, then climbed out first. He looked around and glared, I assumed, at Frank, then reached in to help me.

With a deep breath, I took his hand and allowed him to pull me out. The sight outside of the base surprised me. An army larger than I had previously seen stood out there waiting for me, Frank at the front. So arrogant. Most Kings would be at the back, but he knew neither Louis nor I would risk the lives of anyone to try to take him out.

No one made a sound as I made my way to him, head held high, and Louis at his normal distance behind me. I was glad I had chosen boots because the mud beneath my feet sucked and sloshed at them.

Frank had an irritating, cocky grin plastered on his face. No one had to tell me that he was thinking about the dream last night; that he was thinking about how I boasted I would be taking back my kingdom, and there he stood before me with his army in navy blue behind him.

I stopped in front of him and we stared at each other until his grin straightened out. I didn't know what to expect, but was unsurprised when he reached out and slapped me with his bare hand across the same cheek he had slapped a couple days earlier. Unlike the slap from my dream, it hurt me more than it hurt him, but I didn't give him the satisfaction of making a sound.

Roughly, he grabbed my arm, the one with my crumpled hand attached, and pulled me toward a hover and shoved me in. My hurt hand slammed against the doorway and I cried out in pain, but Frank didn't seem to notice or care. He pushed me in the rest of the way and climbed in behind me, closing the door and leaving Louis standing outside.

The hover took off and I saw some of the army get into military hovers of their own to follow us. Not all of them left, though, which made me nervous for the people inside the base.

"What will you do with the people inside?" I asked.

"I said I would not hurt them and I won't, Rose. But they will be banished. Those who stand against me will not be tolerated any longer."

"Does that include me?"

He quickly reached out again and I instinctively flinched. Pulling his hand back, he said, "Never you, Rose. I will never give you up," The words were spoken softly. He was crazy. He still thought there was some chance that I would fall for him.

Slower this time, he reached over and undid the clasp that held my hair up. With a questioning gaze, he ran his fingers through it and I sat stone-still beneath the smooth stroking. "Where did you get Champoing de Repousse des Cheveux?"

I shrugged, unwilling to give him any information, also irritated that he had known about the product all along.

"I suppose it doesn't really matter. Your little movement is over. You're here with me now and I won't be letting you go again."

I pursed my lips together and he chuckled his annoying chuckle. "I bet you didn't see it coming, did you? Louis betraying you. When are you going to learn, Rose, that everyone has something more important to them than you? Everyone except me, that is." He moved across the seats so he was sitting next to me, and brushed my hair over to my opposite shoulder with his hand.

"Nothing is more important to me than you, Rose." He placed a soft kiss on my neck and I cringed. The kisses continued up to my earlobe, where he stopped to nibble and whisper. "You're mine. Learn that and things will be alright for you."

"Will you honor your agreement with Louis?" I whispered hoarsely, trying to change the subject.

"Yes, yes. He and his little family will be banished, too, however. Can't have someone so loyal to you hanging about. It was a real stroke of luck when my soldiers found his wife and daughter wandering around."

Though his face was much too close for comfort, I turned my face to him and met his icy blue gaze. I thought of Louis' sweet little girl and how excited she was when she got to meet me. "Did you hurt them?" That broke his spell and he jolted back away from me.

"Roots, Rose. I'm not a monster." I raised a brow at him. "Despite what you think. No. I didn't hurt them. I didn't even put them in a prison cell, believe it or not. They were guarded around the clock, but no harm came to them.

"In fact, they were being held in a hover close to where you and Louis came out. I arranged to have soldiers from New California meet them at the border and take them in as refugees."

I couldn't hide the surprise on my face. That he would take such care to ensure Louis and his family made it over the border was wise, to be sure. He didn't want loyalists around, but why was he acting with such concern.

"I don't understand why you care so much that they make it over the border alright, aside from obviously not wanting him around."

Frank examined his cleanly trimmed nails. "I think you've lost enough people that you love, don't you?" He looked at me again, and again I was shocked. "I've told you before, Rose. If there was any other way to accomplish what we wanted, we never would have killed anyone. The last thing I *want* to do is cause you pain."

"Then why do you do it? You say you love me more than anything, but it isn't true, Frank." I made sure to call him by that name, remembering his threat from a couple days ago. "There *is* something you love more: that crown. You desire power more than anything else in this world."

Frank didn't say anything after that for a very long time. For hours, we both looked out opposite windows. The only communication we had were the gentle circles he drew on my shattered hand. It didn't hurt. By that point, my hand had gone numb. I looked forward to Doctor Quincy fixing it.

"You're right," Frank said when we were only a few minutes from Evergreen Palace.

"Pardon?"

"You're right, Rose. I do love power more than you, but not by much."

"Such a comfort, Frank," I muttered.

"I will always be as honest with you as possible. The only reason I told you I loved you more than anything was that I was unaware of it until now. But you're right. I do love power."

Great. Let's add bringing such an atrocious thing to his attention to my list of grave errors.

"I love how I feel when people bow before me as I sit on my illustrious throne. I love commanding the Royal Millerian Army. I love when people beg for their lives, having the power over whether they live or die. I love being King over an entire kingdom. I love being your husband and having you at my command.

"You've fought me for too long, Rose. No more. No more fighting. You will be my Queen. You will show me respect. If you fight me hard enough to lose your legs, you will lose them permanently next time. Am I understood?"

I knew I had to look outrageously perplexed at this burst of self-revelation from Frank. I never expected him to admit such things out loud, no matter how true they were. I wasn't sure if it was scarier before when he was delusional or now that he had this new clarity to his life and he glommed onto it, rather than pushed it away.

He gripped my chin in his hand, brought his face close to mine, and repeated himself. "Am. I. Understood?"

"Yes, Frank," I said meekly.

He grinned with his teeth, making him look a bit like a beast, then bruisingly crushed his lips against mine. He bit at my lips and breathed into my mouth at a disgusting rate. His hands roamed my body and I wanted to die. He didn't let me go until we pulled up to the palace.

Sitting back as if nothing had just happened, he smiled and said, "Now. Let's have Doctor Quincy take a look at your hand, shall we?"

Chapter 21

Unsurprisingly, Frank escorted me up to our room on the top floor and deposited me there, locking the door behind him when he left. I examined the room that used to belong to my parents and wished that something, anything had been left the same. He had changed more while I was gone, even though I hadn't been gone long.

Now, even my window cushion was navy blue instead of ivory. I plopped down on the cushion and watched the rain pelt the window. I couldn't believe I was in captivity again. Freedom was so sweet, and I missed its feeling already.

A short while after I arrived back at the palace, a guard knocked, then opened the door without waiting for a response. Doctor Quincy made his way in and walked over to me while the guard stationed himself just inside the door.

When he got to me, I raised my injured hand to him. Ever so gently, he removed the gauze around my hand and made a wincing expression when he saw what it looked like. "Blossoms and roots, my Queen of Hearts. What happened? Did King Francis do this to you?"

I shook my head. "No. I punched the wall when I learned of Louis' betrayal, and there was no way around coming back here."

"Well, I can't fault you for that, can I?" Doctor Quincy took out a hand-healer and put my hand in it. The device hummed and I felt pressure as it took measurements, then began the mending process. Doctor Quincy cleared his throat. "I thought you should know, my Queen of Hearts, that I have requested to return to Britainnia."

"Oh. I see."

"It is time that I return home and see to the young King there. He has his Great Uncle for a Regent, but, rumor has it there will be a trial of great importance for which I have been called upon to testify."

I knew exactly what trial he meant and it eased the blow of his leaving. "Were you granted your request?"

"Indeed, Your Majesty."

"Will you return after the trial?" I asked.

"I do not rightly know, Queen Miriam. It will depend on what is required of me when I get there."

I nodded and we didn't say anything else as the machine worked its technological magic. Doctor Quincy set my hand, still in the machine, on my lap and went over to read some medical book on the couch. I really shouldn't have been surprised at Doctor Quincy wanting to leave. It made sense. With my escape and return, and the part he played in it, it would be safest for him to leave. Plus, he understandably viewed it as his duty to me and his own kingdom to participate in the trial of Prince Phineas.

Part way through the healing, Frank came back. When he entered, the guard stepped out. Doctor Quincy stood and bowed as Frank stalked over to him. "What did we learn, Doctor?" Frank asked.

"Her hand was quite fractured, sir. It will likely be another half hour before the machine is done fixing her hand."

Frank arrogantly quirked his brow. "Of course it was fractured, Doctor. I would not have sent for you otherwise. Did we learn how it happened?"

Doctor Quincy made the mistake of looking over to me for permission to tell him. Frank slapped him. "Let us be clear, Doctor. *I* am the one ultimately in charge. Not the Queen. If I ask you for information, you will give it to me. Yes?"

"Yes, of course, Your Majesty. Please forgive my disrespect." Doctor Quincy took a shuddering breath, shaken by the violent outburst of the King. I had never seen him hit the doctor, but I couldn't be sure if he actually had or not before this time. "Her hand was, uh, shattered by the force of her punching her wall, sir."

"She punched her wall?"

I hated that they were talking about me as if I wasn't sitting right there, but I didn't dare say anything about it. I had no idea what to expect from this new Frank.

"She said she, uh, punched her wall when she learned of what Louis did and that she would be losing her freedom again."

"I see. You can wait in the Royal Library for word that the machine is finished. I assume it will beep or something?"

"Uh. Yes, Your Majesty."

I could tell he wanted to refuse to leave, but he was feeling the same way I was. Unsure. We both sort of knew what to expect from Frank before, the lovesick, crazy Frank. This power hungry Frank was a completely different beast.

Wordlessly, Doctor Quincy left the room, and I assumed he went to the library as ordered. Frank came over and sat at the edge of my window cushion. "I changed your cushion while you were gone. I knew you liked to sit here, so I got you something softer."

"I noticed."

"Are you afraid of me, Rose?"

"Always."

"Then you won't fight me anymore?"

I stayed quiet. I wanted to fight him desperately, but it all seemed hopeless. He sighed deeply.

"You make no sense to me." He was speaking quietly. Not dangerously quiet. Just quiet. "You say you're afraid of me, but you won't say that you're done fighting."

"There are things that you want of me that I'm not ready to give."

"Your virginity? My children?"

I nodded. He leaned against the wall, looking absurd with half his body hanging off the seat; it wasn't big enough for the two of us. "You think once you've given them up, it's like admitting defeat." I didn't acknowledge that he was absolutely right.

He placed a hand on my calf and began absentmindedly tracing patterns with his fingers. "I've thought of it often, you know. You being round with my child, sitting here in this window reading one of your books of fantasy or a history book of some sort. You would be beautiful pregnant, Rose." He spoke of my greatest nightmare dreamily. "You would be a good mother, too, I think. I don't really remember mine much, but my father always said she was a good woman. Was your mother a good woman, Rose?"

"She was the best," I choked.

"I am sorry she had to die."

"She was in the way of your greatest love."

He hummed in consideration of the thought. It was almost better then, being able to be a hundred percent honest with each other. He wasn't lying to himself anymore. He wasn't trying to convince me that what he wanted was the best for me or the kingdom.

"Rose, I may love my power most of all, but I do still love you." He wanted to move over me and surround me with himself, but he was blessedly blocked by the hand-healer. He stopped trying and plopped back against the wall. "I can't believe you punched the wall when you found out you had to come back to me."

"I didn't have to do anything. I chose to come back to save those people."

"That is beside the point. You really hate me so much that you broke your hand because of your temper."

I thought on that. I had never really hated anyone. I pitied a lot of people, greatly disliked a few, but never hated. Did I hate Frank? "To be honest, Frank. I'm not sure that I actually do hate you. I hate what you've done. I hate what you continue to do. But you, personally? I'm not so sure.

"I've pitied you more than once. I've been afraid of you. I've been angry with you. I've been frustrated and annoyed. But I don't think I hate you. I definitely dislike you, though."

He laughed dryly at the last comment.

"Yes. I did punch the wall," I continued. "But that shouldn't surprise you. Look at everything you've put me through. My imprisonment on your island. The deaths of my loved ones. The mind-bending you performed that night I fought you and won. Why should it surprise you that I would escape and not want to come back?"

"Can I ask you a question?" Frank asked, completely ignoring my tirade.

"You'll ask it whether I want you to or not."

"Did you have sex with Harrison?"

I only laughed.

"What is so funny? It's not an unreasonable assumption that you would. You're in love with him."

When I stopped laughing, I said, "I'll be straightforward with you. I wanted him to marry me that first night I was there. I begged him to. Said the marriage to you couldn't count because it was done under duress. Do you know what he said?" Frank shook his head with a dumbfounded look on his face.

"He said it did count because it was before God, even if the pastor was a traitor. He said we needed to wait until my marriage to you was dissolved officially before he would marry me. So, no. We didn't have sex, Frank. But it was because Harrison was honorable, not me."

"So you would have if he would have let you?"

"I would have if he would have married me."

"We're married. You should stop fighting this."

"Never."

As if on cue, the hand-healer beeped. Frank jumped up and ran to the door like the room was on fire. He gave instructions to one of the guards to get the Doctor, then turned back to me. His stare was studious, as if trying to solve a problem. Suddenly, his face lit up and he rushed out of the door.

I wasn't sure really what to think of that, but I was glad for him to be gone. The night ahead of me would be long and the more time I had to prepare myself, the better.

Chapter 22

Doctor Quincy and the guard came in soon after Frank left and he quickly removed the device. Despite trying not to, I wept when he was ready to leave and he obliged me with a hug. With Doctor Quincy gone, the only one I had left nearby was Marie, and I wasn't even sure that she was still in the palace.

As Doctor Quincy left the room, the guard outside poked his head in and informed me that I would be dining with *King Francis* and an honored guest. I was expected to be ready by 5:00, which was only fifteen minutes from then.

I was sure Frank probably wanted me to change out of my Arborian-colored clothing, but he could just go pull weeds, as much as I cared. Because my boots were covered with mud, I changed out them for a pair of brown heels. With a quick refreshing of mascara and a spritz of hairspray, I was ready to go.

When I knocked on the door I knew was locked, the guard opened it and gave my outfit an appraising look. When his gaze met mine, my expression dared him to question my decision. He gulped, then began to lead the way.

Frank was not taking any chances. To prevent any hope of escape, I had four guards flanking me, arranged like four points of a compass. It was absurd. I could tell he had either banished or killed many people in the palace; it was practically empty, probably like the rest of the kingdom. I did take comfort in knowing he was banishing people to New California, not realizing that they were allies of mine.

As we approached the Dining Hall, I heard muffled conversation between Frank and whoever our guest was. When I was closer I could make out some words.

"How … will it …?" Frank was asking.

"The longest …" There was a long moment when all I could hear was mumbling. "… week, my King," he responded.

Before it could go any further, I came in and they clammed up, making me nervously curious about what they were discussing. What new terror was he getting ready to unleash on my people now?

"Ah. Queen Miriam," Frank said in a formal voice.

So fake.

"Come. Sit, my love." Frank gestured to my seat on his right. To his left was a young man around our age. His dusty blond hair was pulled back in a low ponytail and his goatee was well-groomed. After a moment, I recognized him as one of the men who had publicly made crude sounds at me at the Christmas Ball. Obediently, I went over and sat down in the chair next to Frank.

"And who is our guest, Frank?" I asked, purposefully using his informal title in front of his company. The first course of broccoli cheddar soup was brought out as I sat, and I began eating after my question.

"This is Duke Sandran of Sequoia," Frank introduced. I choked on my soup at the ridiculous name and the man smirked.

"My mother wanted a girl," he said in a smooth tenor. "She wanted to name her Sandra. Not to be deterred by the universe saying 'no,' she kept the name and masculinized it as best as she could."

"I am sorry," I said, not apologizing for my rudeness, but for his cruel mother giving him a name that probably got him teased relentlessly growing up. No wonder he became a man who would side with Frank in all this.

He just chuckled. "No offense taken, my Queen," he said, misunderstanding my apology as I assumed he would. There was something odd about him, but I couldn't put my finger on it.

Frank and Duke Sandran discussed the happenings in Duke Sandran's province. Clean-up in the streets. Banishments of those who were outwardly against the new Crown. The fishermen trying to meet the impossible quotas Duke Sandran had put in place.

As they bored through the conversation, I ate the rest of the meal in silence and sipped at the single glass of Blackberry Moscato I was allowing myself for the night. I had to have my wits about me, I knew. There was no way Frank was going to let the night go by without trying something with me.

Duke Sandran was as cruel as Frank. He talked about how he personally tortured and killed several rebels in an attempt to find the People's Base in his province. Thinking about how the headquarters of the resistance was right under the pompous Duke's nose made me smile without thinking about it.

"Do you find something amusing, my love?" Frank spoke to me for the first time since we sat down all evening.

"Yes," I responded and sipped at my wine again.

The men waited a moment, expecting me to expand, then Frank said, with exasperation, "Do you care to share with us?"

"Not really."

"Will you?"

"If you insist."

"I do."

"Alright, then. It is amusing to me that the headquarters of the resistance was right underneath your friend's nose the whole time. All your torture and murder was pointless because those people are unconditionally loyal to me."

"Except Louis," Frank said coolly, twisting the knife that was Louis' betrayal. The amusement fell from my face and I gulped down the rest of my wine.

Duke Sandran leaned forward on his elbow and cupped his chin in his hand. "Ornery little thing, are you not?" He said to me.

"Disrespectful, are you not?" I quipped. "I am still your Queen."

"You are a figurehead," he retorted.

"Watch your tongue, Sandran," Frank warned, and Duke Sandran stopped speaking. The look of shock he sent Frank told me that Frank was using his ability to stop him from speaking. "You know why you are here. It is not to sit there and insult your Queen. Should *she* decide to insult *you*, she can. She is Queen and it is her prerogative to do so. Understood?"

Duke Sandran nodded and I smirked at him. When his tongue was released, he opened and closed his mouth a few times to loosen the muscles in his jaw. Aside from Frank, this man had to be the biggest jerk I had ever met.

With a sigh, Frank sat back and gave me that studious look again. "My Rose," he muttered, as if to himself. "You've left me no choice, my love." Glancing at Duke Sandran, he said under his breath, "Go ahead."

Duke Sandran's face lit up with the grin of a psychopath, and I squirmed in my seat. "Frank?" I said nervously, but he only looked at me with a tinge of regret.

"Frank is so lucky to have you," Duke Sandran said, his voice smoothing over me like a warm breeze in Atlantis. Why was his voice such a nice thing to listen to?

I shook my head at the unusual comparison running through my head and said, "Luck had nothing to do with it."

"You are absolutely right. She is right, of course, King Francis. It was fate was it not?"

"Fate?" My head was beginning to feel foggy. I glanced at my empty wine glass.

I only had one, right?

"Fate, yes, my Queen. Fate brought you together."

"I – I'm not sure I believe in fate."

"No matter. Fate, the universe, God. You two were meant to be."

"Meant to be," I repeated.

I looked over at Frank, whose face remained emotionless. Duke Sandran was talking about us. Why wasn't he responding, too?

My brain was screaming something was wrong. That Duke Sandran must be a siren like Lucas. I tried to shake out of it, but couldn't. Perhaps my mind was still weak from Frank's attack not long before or maybe the siren's power was just one that trumped my own abilities. After all, Frank was susceptible to Lucas even from several floors below him.

I honestly couldn't tell you the exact moment I lost the battle, but when I did, I felt an instant calm. Everything was going to be okay. I didn't need to fight anymore.

"Your love is a testament to us all, Your Majesty. The way you have been able to forgive and forget is inspirational."

I flushed. "Well, I don't know about that."

"Oh. It absolutely is. Tell me, when can we expect a little Prince or Princess to be playing about the palace?"

"Uh – I – Uh." I looked to Frank for help. It seemed like kind of a rude question, and I wasn't sure how to answer it anyway, especially considering the fact we hadn't consummated our marriage yet.

"We are not expecting yet, Duke Sandran, but hopefully soon," answered Frank, reaching over and gently taking my hand.

"Yes," I agreed with a smile. "Hopefully soon."

Chapter 23

Duke Sandran, that nice man, left soon after our conversation about children. Frank and I walked up to our room hand-in-hand and I pondered the discussion.

Why haven't I given myself to Frank? He is my husband, after all. How cruel of me to withhold myself for so long.

When we got to the room, Frank locked the door behind him, as usual. I didn't waste time. I sashayed over to him, grabbed his handsome face in my hands and kissed him. He grunted in surprise, but quickly wrapped his arms around me and pulled me closer to him.

He was gentle, so gentle with me, knowing it was my first time. I couldn't figure out why I had been so afraid of him, of doing that with him. He worshipped me in a way I knew no other man could. When we were done, he cleaned me up and held me close to him, whispering words of accolades and love against the back of my neck, pressing soft kisses there between his words.

I couldn't remember a time in my life when I felt so loved, so cherished. Frank loved me. He was all I had left in the world and I would live my life trying to please him, to show him I loved him as much, if not more than he loved me.

I turned over so I was facing him and he brushed stray strands of hair out of my face. He was so handsome with his chiseled facial structure, dark hair, and eyes the color of the sky on a winter's day. I knew he had done horrible things, but did he really have a choice? I certainly hadn't helped him achieve the greatness he so rightfully deserved. Really, the deaths of all my people, friends, and family were my own fault. Not his.

"Frank?"

"Hmm?"

"I'm sorry."

He furrowed his brow in confusion. "For what, Rose?"

"For everything." I traced the line of his face from his cheek to the tip of his chin. "It's all my fault, really. All those deaths."

He brushed his lips against mine. "No, my love. That wasn't your fault. That was me. I've done horrible things, but there's no need for any of that ugliness anymore, right?"

"No. I'll help you make things right. It's the least I can do."

Frank pulled me against his body in an embrace and tucked my head under his chin. "We've begun the healing process for us tonight, my love. You just get some sleep now and we'll begin healing our kingdom in the morning."

"Yes. Sleep sounds good. It's been a long day."

I let him hold me as we drifted off to sleep. He fell asleep first and I tried to match the rhythm of my breathing with his.

I open my eyes and find not Frank, but Prince Harrison sharing the bed with me. We're fully clothed in our pajamas. I jump out of the bed.

"What are you doing here?" I demand.

He looks at me like I have two heads. "I miss you, Rose. I was checking on you to make sure you're alright."

"I'm fine. Now leave."

He sits up straight in the bed. "What?"

I try to send him away. "Why isn't it working?"

He stands up and starts to walk over to me, but stops when I back up. "It's not working because I'm a mind-reader, Rose. You know that. I'll leave when I figure out what is going on here and how to fix it."

"There's nothing to figure out, Prince Harrison."

"What's with the 'Prince'?"

I sigh. "It's over, Harrison. We've lost. I'm moving on. It's time that I love Frank the way he loves me. He is my husband."

"Have you completely lost it?"

"No. I've never been clearer."

"Hold on." He takes a few deep breaths. "Walk me through your day after you left the base with Frank."

"I don't see how that will help anything, Harrison."

"Twisting tornados, Rose! Just give me a run through of your sand-blastin' day!" He shouts at me. He never shouts at me or uses the curse words of Southland.

"Fine. He bragged in the hover the whole way back to Evergreen Palace and admitted that he loves his power more than me. That really stings by the way. After everything we've been through –"

"Rose, focus."

"Fine. Doctor Quincy came and put my hand in a hand-healer, and Frank and I had a heart-to-heart while my hand was healing. I was very unkind to him. I'm so lucky he still cares."

"Rose," he begged, drawing out my name.

I huff. "Later on, we had dinner with Duke Sandran of Sequoia and –"

"Wait. What?"

"Please listen. We had dinner with Duke Sandran of Sequoia and –"

"Sand-blastin' twistin' tornados!" Harrison shouts.

"What on Earth is your problem? I know he can be unpleasant, but once you get to know him he isn't all that bad."

"He's a rooting siren, Rose. Like Lucas."

I let that sink in. "He's a siren?"

"Yes. I can tell he's messed with your mind, too."

"Don't be absurd. Don't you think I would know if my brain had been poked at?"

"Obviously not."

"What makes you say that it has?" I challenge.

"You're essentially telling me you're in love with Frank and not me."

"Just because I'm finally allowing myself to feel what I feel doesn't mean anyone's been in my head ... besides you, of course. How do I know it wasn't Lucas planting all those thoughts in my head about you all this time? You have been friends for a while, apparently."

"Oh, please." Harrison says, but stops himself from going further. "This is bad. There's no convincing you of anything right now. I have to get to you before you do something you'll regret later."

"I will regret nothing. I love him."

Harrison's face blanches. "No. Please, no. Please tell me you didn't."

"I did. And I don't regret it."

Harrison blinks at me and clenches his fists. "I'm gonna kill him," he mutters and disappears.

I climb back in the bed and go back to sleep, hoping that is the last I ever see of Prince Harrison of Southland.

Chapter 24

The next morning, Frank helped me get ready, kissing my neck as he buttoned up my navy blue dress in the back. Since he was helping me, I assumed that meant Marie was gone. Oh well. She was with the traitors anyway.

While I sat at my vanity to do my hair and makeup, he sat on the sofa and watched with a goofy grin on his face. When I was done, I looked over to him and asked him, "What are you looking at that is so funny?"

"Nothing is funny, Rose. You're just beautiful and I can't believe I finally have you. It's everything I dreamed it would be and more."

I walked over to him and sat in his lap, draping my arms around his neck and giving him a kiss. "I should have given in to you a long time ago, Frank. I'm so sorry I wasted so much time."

"No more apologies, my love. We'll look forward from now on, yes?"

"Alright."

"I wish I could just sit here all day with you in my arms, but we have to go down to the Throne Room to hold Court."

I traced an idle pattern on his chest. "Do we really? I can think of much better things to do."

We were late for Court. Very late for Court. But if anyone cared, no one said anything. A couple of the guards gave Frank knowing glances. In the past, it would have bothered me, but I was proud of my husband now, and proud of our endeavor to bring our heir into the world.

Milleria would become a proud nation, especially now that the rebels were gone. Frank sat in his thorn-engraved throne and I sat in my floral one. Now that I wasn't harboring bitterness and anger toward my love, I could see they were quite beautiful. The artist really put a lot of love and work into them.

"Frank, my love?"

"Yes, my Queen?"

"Do you think we could get the carpenter who made our thrones to make the baby's cradle when it comes time? These really are quite lovely."

Frank took my hand in his and kissed it. "Of course, Rose. Anything for you." He made a gesture with his hand for the guard to bring in our first case of the day. Imagine my surprise when it was Marie who was dragged before us.

Frank tsked. "Marie, Marie, Marie. Traitor to the first Crown, now traitor to me. Whatever shall we do with you? What do you think, Queen Miriam? Hmm? Death or banishment?"

Marie looked at me with wide, unbelieving eyes. "What?"

"Silence!" Frank shouted. When he spoke to me again, he did so softly. "What do you think, Rose?"

While I was completely in support of my husband, I still didn't have the stomach to order someone's death. I also didn't want to sentence even more people to Frank's wrath, so I didn't tell him about who was allied with the rebels and the Queen of Southland. We could overcome anything they threw at us anyway.

"Banishment. To New California."

"As you wish." Frank seemed disappointed with the lack of bloodshed, but honored my decision and gestured her out of the room. The guards dragged her back out. I tried not to look at the tears of betrayal in her eyes. Well, now she knew how I felt when she betrayed me.

The rest of the day was spent listening to reports by simpering Nobles. I sincerely doubted things were as great as they all made them out to be, but let Frank rule how he would. Some of them, he called out. Others, he let slip by. It seemed as though every one of the Nobles was there that day. All except Duke Robert.

It wouldn't surprise me if Harrison contacted him after the dream and told him his ludicrous theory that Duke Sandran had messed with my head. The claim that the man was a siren wouldn't shock me; his voice had been soothing with its tenor, but I sincerely doubted he had changed my mind about anything.

On our way to dinner, I looked at all the blues, ivories, and browns around the palace. While they weren't colors that I was used to, they were very beautiful. In the center of the dining table was the largest bouquet of blue and white roses I had ever seen. As we passed them to get to our seats, I stopped and smelled them; they smelled as lovely as they looked.

We ate in companionable silence, mainly because I was struggling with whether or not to give away Robert. It would hurt Frank to learn that his friend was actually his enemy and I didn't want to hurt him. I decided to wait until later when we were back in the room.

As I was sipping on my wine after our meal, I had my first vision in a long time.

An image. Frank and Harrison fighting with swords, of all things. Upon Frank's head sat the Crown of Milleria, adorned with blue gems. Harrison wore the King's Crown of Arboria, shining with emeralds and diamonds. Their faces alight with anger and angst.

Though there was nothing particular that said it, I knew that it was a final battle. A time would soon come when Frank and Harrison would face off. Whoever won that fight would determine the future of Arboria.

When I came out of the vision, my wine glass was on the floor and I had somehow missed splashing it on my dress. Frank rushed over to my side and caught me before I slumped out of my chair.

"Are you alright?" he asked.

I wanted to tell him about my vision, but he didn't know about my having visions, in general. Though I loved him with everything, something inside told me not to let him know about the vision. Not even to let him know about my gift at all.

Smiling, I said, "Yes, yes. I'm fine. Just a little tipsy, I think." To help relieve his worry, I said, "Can we dance, dear?"

Complimenting my smile with one of his own, Frank stood, walked over to a holocomm, and put on some modern music channel. A ballad was playing and he held out his hand so we could dance together. As we danced, he looked at me like I was his greatest treasure.

"You've been very quiet today, Rose," he said to me as we twirled around the Dining Hall.

"I've been deep in thought today."

"What about?"

I bit my bottom lip. "I know some things I think you should know, but I'm afraid to tell you. I – I don't want to anger you." Absentmindedly, I removed my hand on his arm and pressed it to my tender cheek. When I had done my makeup, I managed to cover up the bruise, but it still hurt.

Frank placed his hand over mine and we stopped dancing. "I wish I didn't have to do that, but you do understand why I did, don't you?"

I nodded vigorously. "Oh. Yes. Of course, I do, Frank. I have been so very awful to you. I deserve much worse. You have been so patient and merciful to me over the last few months."

"Well, things are different now, so you have nothing to fear from me. Why don't you tell me what you've been thinking, hmm?"

"Well, there are a couple things. Can we go upstairs for this? I don't want to have this conversation here."

"Absolutely."

Gingerly, he took my hand and we made our way upstairs. We didn't get to talking until around an hour later when we were done loving each other and resting in our bed. I rested my hands on his broad shoulder and chest as he traced idly up and down my side.

"You distracted me," Frank murmured with a grin.

"I couldn't help myself," I sighed.

"Blossoms. How I've longed to hear such things from your lips." I blushed when he said it. "Now, about these things you know."

"Well, first of all, you should know that Duke Robert is working with the resistance."

He was quiet for a moment and his lips pressed in a straight line. "Robert?"

"Yes. I assume that's why he wasn't here today to give his report."

"He commed this morning saying he was ill and wouldn't be to Court for a few days."

"I doubt he's coming back."

"How would he even know you've had a change of heart, though? You didn't warn him, did you?"

My eyes widened.

"Of course not. Not you."

I relaxed.

"I didn't warn him, but – well, that's the other thing."

Frank's hand stopped moving and he held my hip instead. "What other thing?"

I cleared my throat. "Harrison came into my dream last night."

Frank's grip tightened and he growled. "You mean to tell me the dream-walking thing is real? That was real when you pulled me into your dream the other night?"

His hand was starting to hurt and I shifted to try to loosen his grasp. That didn't work. "Well, yeah. I thought you knew. I thought that was why you slapped me."

Frank hopped out of bed and began pacing the room, running his hand through his hair. Rubbing my hip, I turned so I was sitting up in bed. "Frank?"

"I can't believe this is happening." He stopped and assessed me. "How long have you been able to do this?"

I shrugged. "Since I woke up from my freeze, I suppose. Frank, please come sit down. I'm sorry about last night. Harrison was erratic and he had some really crazy ideas."

Frank plopped himself down next to me and held my face tightly in his hands. I couldn't have been very attractive with him squishing my face like that, but he didn't seem to care at that moment. "Rose. Tell me what you said to him."

"Ah canth thalk," I muffled through my puckered lips. He lessened his hold and rubbed my cheeks as if to help them relax again. "Thank you. Frank, I know you're concerned about all this, but you need to calm down. You're hurting me left and right."

Frank glanced down at my hip, where his fingerprints were beginning to bruise there. He took a deep breath. "It is very important that you tell me what you told him."

"I told him not to come into my dreams anymore because I was in love with you and the war was over. He wasn't very happy with that and demanded to know everything that happened after we left. I told him about our trip back to the palace and our visit from Duke Sandran." I laughed. "Harrison had this insane idea that Sandran is a siren and used his gift on me." I laughed harder.

Frank chuckled. "Anything else?"

"Uh. Yes. He asked me if I had given myself to you. I said I had and he said he was going to kill you." Frank grunted, so I quickly added, "Not that you need to worry about that, honey. You're well-guarded and your ability would stop him, right?"

Frank gulped. "I need to take a walk." He hopped up from the bed again and quickly pulled his pants and shirt on.

Beginning to take off my blankets to get up, I said, "I'll join you, honey."

Frank rushed over to stop me by gently pushing me back down and covering me back up. "No, no, no. I'm fine. I just need a bit."

"Are you mad at me?" I asked, feeling nervous about his strange behavior. I knew Harrison visiting my dream would upset him, but I didn't expect him to get so shaken up about it. "I didn't mean to do anything wrong. I didn't bring him to my dream, he came to it. We used to visit each other all the time. He knows the way there."

After a quick kiss on my forehead, Frank said, "Not mad at you, love. Just need to think. I'll be back in a bit. You just try to get some rest."

Before I could say "okay," Frank was out the door. He didn't even bother to put on shoes or run a comb through his hair. Was he scared of Harrison? Could Harrison get past the guards and hurt him? Or was Frank actually mad at me, but didn't want to say anything, since things were going so well?

I didn't know, but my mind raced as I lay there in bed staring at the ceiling, now dimly lit green since I gave Frank the code to change the light color on the Space Needle. It was a silly thing to keep from him. Frank wanted the power to be King and I loved him, so I would help him as much as I could in the future. No more pushing his buttons or keeping secrets.

Of course, now that I knew he loved power more than me, I hurt a little. I supposed I deserved it. I fought for too long; it was only natural for him to turn to something else to take priority in his life. I was lucky he hadn't turned to any number of women in his movement, that he hadn't replaced me.

My heart broke a little more at the thought. Perhaps if I worked extra hard, I could earn my way back to the first place in his life. Deciding that I would give him all the information on the resistance that I knew in the morning, I set my mind to falling asleep.

Chapter 25

I hum as I swing in the sofa swing in my rose maze. The sun shines above me through the glass, the drops of rain leftover from earlier causing rainbows to shine all over the room. Life is peaceful now that I have given myself over to Frank. Now that I have learned to trust in him and his love for me.

"My Queen of Hearts," says a familiar voice.

I tipped my head forward at my guest. Or should I say guests. Harrison has his hand on Lucas Flowers' shoulder. I'm guessing that's how he managed to bring him here. Trying to not get angry, I look back up to the transparent ceiling and proceed to ignore them.

"I know you can hear me, my Queen of Hearts," Lucas tries again.

Sighing, I look back to him. "Very well. What is it that you want, Lucas? I don't appreciate uninvited guests in my mind. That goes for you, too, Harrison. I told you last night not to come back. Frank wasn't very happy when I told him about your visit."

"You told him?" Harrison asks me with a flabbergasted tone and expression on his beautiful face.

"Of course I told him," I respond. "He is my husband. There are no secrets between us."

"Except that he's using mind-control to make you love him."

I scoff. "That's preposterous. His ability doesn't work that way."

"His doesn't, but Duke Sandran's does."

"Not this again," I mutter.

Harrison pushes Lucas forward so he can get closer to me. Because of that action, I guess if he releases him, Lucas disappears. Why is he here anyway?

"It's the sand-blastin' truth, Rose. I know you don't believe me. That's why Lucas is here."

"What? So he can siren his way into my mind and convince me of your lies again?"

"My lies?"

"Harrison, she doesn't know what she's saying right now," Lucas says, trying to pacify Harrison's growing ire.

"I know exactly what I'm saying. I'm under no illusion. Frank loves his power more than me. He has said as much, but at least he's honest about it." I stand up and strut right up to the tall Southlander. "You pretend to love me because you know there is no other way you will ever be King of anything. You're a second-born, an extra. Why did your parents even have you?"

Hurt spreads over Harrison's face and Lucas shifts his feet awkwardly. "I'm gonna let that go, darlin', on account that you're not yourself right now. But I'm gonna recommend you shut your mouth before you say anythin' else you will later regret."

The fact that Harrison's accent thickened tells me that he's getting close to losing his temper. I smirk and back off, sitting back on my sofa swing.

"I can't handle this anymore," Harrison says. "Lucas, do your thing."

Out of nowhere, a guitar appears in Lucas' hands. I wonder if he needs to sing for his gift to work. I try to send them away before he opens his mouth, but I can feel Harrison fight me. Lucas begins to sing.

"Return to us,
Our Queen of Hearts.
Be reminded,
Our Queen of Hearts.
This is not you,
Our Queen of Hearts.
You're better than this,
Our Queen of Hearts."

The lyrics leave much to be desired, but I don't think that's the point of the song. It doesn't matter that it doesn't rhyme, or, rather, that the rhythm is practically nonexistent. What matters is that as he continues to play and sing, something switches in my mind.

Gradually, I become aware of the levels Frank has stooped to, that Harrison wasn't lying to me. Duke Sandran must be a siren and he has used his ability on me. Tears fill my eyes as I realize what I have done. I think about what I did with Frank and the state of our relationship. I exiled Marie. I outed Robert Casey. Frank now knows about my dream-walking. And I gave him –

I bring my hands up to my face and weep openly into them. The music suddenly stops and I feel Harrison kneel before me. He grabs my hands and wraps them around him, bringing me into a comforting embrace.

"Oh, God!" I cry out, sincerely repentant before the One who placed me in authority over my kingdom. "What have I done? What have I done?"

I continue to repeat it like a chant, lamenting all I had done in the name of my love for Frank, a love that was never real. How long was Frank intending to keep me in that state of mind? Forever? Until he successfully got me pregnant?

217

Harrison rubs circles on my back, hushing and shushing, letting me cry into his neck. Eventually, my sobs turn to sniffles and I pull away just enough to look Harrison in his eyes.

"I'm so sorry for everything, Harrison. I'm so sorry for what I said and what I did. I'll understand if you want nothing to do with me." I am really afraid that he will decide to be done with me. I am more trouble than I deserve.

Cupping my face in his hands, he gently says, "I don't blame you for any of it. None of it is your fault. Do you really think I would have gone through all this trouble if I was done with you? I love you, Rose. Nothing will change that. And this isn't your fault. It's Frank's fault. He's a treasonous little jerk and he will pay for everything he's done to you and our kingdom."

"Our kingdom? You still want to marry me?"

"More than anything."

"What if –" I hate to voice it, lest it be true. "He raped me, Harrison – What if I'm carrying his child?"

"You mean my *child?" He smiles and I don't understand what he means. "Rose, any baby you have, I will love. Whether its biological father is Frank or me. It's not its fault, or* your *fault if it is* Frank's, *how it was conceived. He or she will be loved. I swear it."*

"You're too good for me." My eyes start welling with tears again. "Seriously, Harrison. You're like the romance novel man who doesn't exist in reality. What did I do to deserve you?"

"Well, I suppose I am *pretty awesome."*

I slap his arm playfully and he brings me in for another embrace. I don't know how long we stay like that, just being in each other's presence, but eventually, I know it's time for me to wake up.

"What are we going to do?" I ask.

"I can't tell you. Just in case Frank uses Duke Sandran on you again."

I bite my lower lip. "What am I going to do? I can't continue to give myself to him."

Harrison sighs. "Do your best to make him think Duke Sandran's work is still lasting. Hopefully, we'll have you out of there before it becomes a real concern."

I jerked myself awake at the sound of Frank yelling at the guards at the door. Because I couldn't understand a word he was saying, I was assuming he was drunk. The room was no longer green with the light of the Space Needle, but bright with the oranges and pinks of the dawning sun.

Before he entered, I needed to center myself. I recalled those acting classes that had come in handy before and prepared to become that actress again. Telling myself that none of what would happen was real, but a scene in a movie, I got out of bed and put on a robe.

Shuffling over to the door, I murmured, "I'm a famous actress. I can do this." I stopped and stared at the door, listening to the slurred tirade of Frank on the other side. Playing the weak damsel I had been over the last couple of days, I knocked hesitantly on the door from my side. Frank stopped yelling and opened the door.

His appearance was shockingly terrible. His eyes were bloodshot and his hair was sticking out in every direction. Quietly, I said, "Is everything alright, Frank? You seem disturbed."

The guards gave me looks that said, "Go figure, Sherlock." Frank just looked me up and down really quickly and pushed past me into the room. The door slid closed and I watched him pace the room again.

"Frank, please talk to me. I've been worried about you all night."

He sighed and placed his hands on his hips, stopping in front of the window. Even though every instinct told me to make a run for it, I walked over behind him and wrapped my arms around him from behind. Quite easily, it was the most disgusting hug I ever had. He was sweaty and I could smell the alcohol on his breath from behind him.

Frank brought one of my hands to his lips to kiss it and I suppressed a shiver. "Just concerned is all, Rose. Don't worry about it."

"Talk to me, Frank. I can't help you if you don't talk to me."

Frank released my hand, turned around in my arms, and pressed his lips together as he considered what I said. Nonchalantly, I brought my hand under his shirt so it was pressing his skin. I wanted the truth of what he was feeling. The best way was to get the memory straight from his head.

I know I look a mess. I'm not even wearing shoes. Duke Sandran appraises my appearance over the holocomm and I shoot him a dirty look. How dare he look at me like that?

"Remember your place, Sandran. I gave you your title. I can take it away. You deserve more than that for missing the rotting resistance headquarters being right under your nose."

"Of course, Your Majesty. My apologies. I have just never seen you look so –" he wisely doesn't finish that thought.

"How long will it last?" I ask him. He's already told me a million times, but I need reassurance.

"As I have said before, my King, it should last around a week."

"Have you ever had anyone overcome it?"

Sandran quirks a brow at me. "Do you have thoughts that the Queen is coming out of it already? If so, I can make my way there and speak with her again."

"No. She is still the loving wife I always wanted. I am just concerned. I have had some things come to light that I had not expected."

"Oh? And what would that be?"

Should I tell him? I don't see how there's any other choice. "She is a dream-walker. Prince Harrison visited her in her dreams last night."

Sandran's eyes widen. "That is unexpected. Is Prince Harrison a siren, too?"

"No. I do not know. I think if he was, he would have tried to change her last night. Do you agree?"

"Well, yes. That would be what I would do in his position."

There's a large pause in our conversation as I think it through. "Hypothetically, if he was to get a siren to her somehow, could he or she undo what you did?"

"To be honest, my King, I do not know. There is no precedence for it. However, I suppose it is possible."

"Have you seen any movement from the People's Base? Have they evacuated yet?"

"As far as we have seen, they are all still at the base. No one has come or gone from the door that we know about."

"Do you think they have left another way?"

Sandran shrugs. "It is possible, my King. As there is no way for us to know about the layout of the base, there is no way for us to know if they have left by any other exit."

But there is a way for us to know the layout. Rose has been there. She can tell me. She'll be happy to tell me. I can tell she's already jealous of my power and trying to be most important to me. She should have tried sooner.

"Thank you. Keep watching them. I will let you know when your services are needed again up here."

Duke Sandran bows his head. "Anything for you and Milleria, Your Majesty." His face disappears off the comm.

Now to find Rose and get some information. I have to look disheveled so she's concerned for me. It will be the best way to ensure she'll betray her old friends. With Duke Sandran's help, Rose will be wrapped around my finger indefinitely.

Chapter 26

I moved my hand back to the outside of his shirt when the memory ended. Glad that my cheek was pressed against his chest, I ground my teeth together to stop the outburst of anger just dying to be let out.

Although I already knew it, thanks to Lucas, I now knew everything Harrison had assumed was true. Indeed, Frank had used Duke Sandran to make me fall in love with him. The fact that anyone had an ability that strong was terrifying; it also made me glad that we had someone like Lucas on our side to undo whatever horrible things Duke Sandran would do.

Why hadn't Frank used Duke Sandran earlier? I figured it was something similar to the fact that he liked to convince people to do what he wanted rather than use his own ability. I focused on my breathing to keep myself from lashing out at him. He didn't feel any regret at all about his deception, about everything he had taken from me. It wasn't enough for him to take my kingdom and kill everyone I held dear. He had to take my virginity, too. Was nothing sacred?

Belying the way I was feeling, I pulled back and gave him a soft smile. "Alright. You don't have to tell me if you don't want to," I said and pecked his lips with mine. I began to pull back, but he held me firm.

"You're not still in love with him are you?" he asked.

Pretending not to know what he was talking about, I said, "In love with who? You're the only man for me, Frank. You should know that by now."

He traced the outlines of my face with a finger. "It's only been a couple days since you gave yourself completely to me, since we've stopped warring against each other. I know you've loved Harrison for some time now. I just want to make sure that's a thing of the past."

Capturing his hand with mine, I turned my head into his palm and pressed a kiss into it. "You are the only one for me now, Frank. Only you."

Frank sighed heavily and I knew his questions were coming, the ones he was acting out-of-sorts for. "I have a question for you and I'm not sure how you'll react to it. I know you have friends at the People's Base in Sequoia, but my people tell me they have seen no activity from the only exit we know of. I hate to ask it of you, to betray your friends, but I have to know. Are there any other exits that they could have used to leave or are they disobeying my order and staying there?"

I looked at him aghast. "Frank, I can't believe you would ask me such a question. Wait. Yes, I can." I stepped away from his arms and stood in front of the empty fireplace, staring at it as if a crackling fire filled its cavern.

"I understand your hesitation –"

"Do you? I know what you do to traitors, Frank. I love you. You know that, but I can't be a part of any more death." I matched the heavy sigh he had performed before. "Fortunately, there isn't much for me to tell anyway. I wasn't there for long, only a couple of nights, before you came for me. I didn't get a tour or anything. Harrison was going to do that soon, I suppose, but we didn't get around to it.

"The only exit I know of is the one I took to walk out to you." Lie. "I'm not sure there are any other ones." Another lie. "However, it wouldn't surprise me if there *were* other exits. It would only make sense." I purse my lips as I felt his approach. "Please don't ask me these questions anymore."

Frank wrapped his arms around me and looked pleadingly into my eyes. "I will try not to, but you have to understand, Rose. I have to squash this resistance before it grows too large. You're probably safe because the people love you, but I know I'm dead if they manage to get here somehow."

"I understand."

After a kiss on the cheek, he spoke softly into my ear. "I want to be there for you and our children. I want to watch them grow and become powerful men and women in this world. I want to grow old with you. But none of that will be possible if I'm dead."

"I want all that, too," I replied with forced tears in my eyes. Tears were easy to conjure after everything I had been through. While my false life sat in the gap of the missing ten years of my real life, I still found this life hard to grasp.

Only a few months ago, I was a widowed mother, raising my little Harmony. I closed my eyes and pictured her bouncing curls and laughing smile. She was my whole world, my biggest and best responsibility.

Now, she was gone. Even though I knew it was foolish to feel it, I felt like I had failed her. My only job was to ensure her safety and happiness, and she didn't even exist anymore. No. She never really existed at all.

I went from widowed mother to blossoming Princess to struggling Queen in a matter of months. No longer did I fight the nightmares of my daughter, but the real monsters who sought to destroy or conquer everything I love.

Because of all that, I was able to produce the tears to convince Frank that what he said meant anything to me. I loathed the idea of having to spend the rest of my days in Frank's arms. Of him fathering my children and raising them to become monsters just like him. Just like his father did to him.

I didn't know what happened to his mother. He had never shared that with me, but I knew she no longer lived. Because of High General Miller's rank, the whole Royal family had attended her memorial service when Frank was a small boy. I wondered briefly what she was like, and what Frank would have been like if she was still around. Did his father lose it after she died or was he always a traitor to the Crown?

Frank wiped my tears with the pad of his thumb as he trailed kisses down my jaw to my mouth. When his lips met mine, I couldn't help the shudder that racked through my body. I only hoped he took it as a shudder of pleasure, rather than one of revulsion.

Pulling away, but staying close, he said, "With your help, I will be here, my love. I will always be here for you and our children. For our kingdom." Moving his hand to the small of my back, he pulled me closer to him.

Concerned that our nonverbal conversation was leading somewhere I didn't want to go, I cautiously pulled away from him. Although I expected him to hang on, he released me and relaxed his posture, letting out a big yawn in the process. Making my way to the closet, I said, "If you need some sleep, dear, I can take Court this morning alone. You look positively ragged from whatever it was that kept you up all night."

"No. I don't want you to have to do that alone," he responded. He wasn't fooling anyone. I knew his real reason was that he didn't want me doing it alone at all. That would mean giving up some of his power to me.

Disrobing in the closet and changing into day clothes, I said, "Well, how about we just cancel Court for the morning, then?" He was quiet in the other room, which gave me confidence that he was considering my idea. I just hoped he would take the bait for the rest. When I was finished dressing, I walked out of the closet. Frank was in bed, nearly asleep.

As I quickly applied some makeup and threw my hair up into a bun, I said, "I was thinking. It might be good for me to walk around Petrichoria this morning. I think it may go a long way for people to see me happy on my own, rather than always by your side. Perhaps I can convince them that you're right for our kingdom."

He thought about my proposal with heavy lids. "Hmm. You may be right, love." Frank grabbed my hand and gently led me to the door. When we were out of the room, Frank ordered the four guards there to escort me into town and to grab a couple other ones on the way out.

Trying to hide how ecstatic I was that he was letting me out of the palace, even if it was with a large escort, I pulled him back into the room and shut the door behind us. After walking with him over to the bed, I tucked the blankets tightly around his body. Kissing his forehead, I said, "I'll see you when I return."

He yawned again. "Yes, love. Then we can spend some time in your garden."

"That sounds lovely, dear," I said, gliding out of our room. I didn't know how I was going to escape these guards, but it was going to happen. I was done being a victim. It was time for me to become a victor.

Chapter 27

Demurely, I walked down the steps of the Core and out the front door with my six guards. The trail from the door to the gate was long, but I didn't mind. Taking my time, I took in the view, breathed in the fresh air, and tried to figure out how I was going to find the Petrichorian People's Base after getting around these guards. Once I got there, I was sure I would be able to contact Harrison somehow to let him know I successfully left Evergreen Palace.

When I got to the gate, the guards didn't even blink before opening them for me. As they both bowed respectfully, I nodded my acknowledgement, then strode down the street. Because it was still relatively early, a lot of shops were still closed, but a few were open. From a nearby bakery, for example, I smelled the aroma of fresh bread.

As I inhaled my newly found freedom, I noticed I had stopped in front of my grocer. Ever since I was a small child, I loved coming to Hank and Anna's Grocer when we visited Petrichoria.

If only I could get away, I know they would shelter me.

Continuing on, I encountered a few people, who bowed or curtseyed and quickly proceeded on their intended path, likely not wanting anything to do with the guards. Several stores down from the grocers, I came across what I thought could be my saving grace.

Several mannequins adorned in a variety of corsets in varying shades of red lined the window display. I paused in front of the window and looked at them for what I knew to be an uncomfortable amount of time for my male guards. When one of them coughed into his hand, I went in for the kill.

"I think I'm going to go in. Come on," I waved with my hand for them to join me, but they didn't move.

"Um. Your Majesty," one of them said. "Couldn't you come back another time? Perhaps when King Francis is available to be with you?"

Turning around, I placed my hands on my hips and furrowed my brows at him. "Are you questioning me?"

"No, of course not – "

"Because while I might not be the one with the most power in this kingdom, I certainly come in a close second and I definitely have a higher ranking than you."

"Your Majesty – "

"Now, I am going into that shop with or without you. What is it going to be?"

I watched as the gears turned in his head. The inner battle of whether to follow orders, even into the lacy land of feminine horror, or to flake out and face Frank's wrath was amusing to me, but I kept a straight face.

He looked to his compatriots, who were not any help to him. Based on the fact that they were waiting on his decision told me he was their leader, even though his stripes on his uniform declared him to be the same rank as them.

The leader sighed and said to the others, "Alright. You two, go around to the back and guard that door. You two, check the sides of the buildings for any other exits and stand there if you find any. If you don't, split up. One of you goes to the back, the other joins us out front." Looking back to me, he said, "We'll be right out here if you need anything, Your Majesty."

That translates to "don't try anything funny."

Nodding to him, I strutted to the door and it opened automatically. The young woman behind the counter walked up to me. "Welcome, is there anything I can –" Then she realized who I was and dipped into a curtsey.

"Please stand. You don't need to do that with me," I said.

"I would be remiss to not demonstrate the respect you deserve," she said, then added in a deliberate manner, "My Queen of Hearts.

Not believing my luck in serendipitously finding someone in the Resistance, I asked loudly, "Are these all your offerings or do you have anything made of finer materials in the back?"

"We have many luxurious offerings in the back. I simply have not put them out yet. They sell out rather quickly, you see," she responded.

Noting the guard watching me from the outside, I gave him a little wave of my fingers. Blushing, he turned forward again.

"Can you show me?" I asked.

"Yes, Your Majesty."

The young woman brought me to the back. "Quickly, we have to go before they begin to suspect anything."

"They're guarding all the exits. There's no way out, but you need to get something to Prince Harrison for me. I –"

"Beg your pardon, Madam, but there is another way." Lifting a rug, she revealed a trap door. I openly gaped at it, then looked back to her smug face. "All the shops are connected underground," she began as she hustled me down the ladder. "Only one shop has a tunnel to the People's Base, though. I'll take you there."

She did a dance of tugging and pulling at the rug so it fell back over the door when she shut it. As soon as it was dark again, dim lights that lined the walls turned on. Speedily, we made our way down the tunnel until we stopped and climbed another ladder into the storage area of a different shop.

"Stay here," she whispered and left.

I looked around and noted meats, produce, dairy, and household supplies on shelves throughout the room. Just as I deduced I was in the back area of the grocer, the young woman came in with Anna. She was a friendly woman, which was why I entrusted her with Rose's care.

"How did you –" She stopped herself again and I couldn't help but widen my smile. "You escaped." It wasn't a question.

"Indeed." I folded my hands in front of me.

"How? From the pictures I have seen and the rumors I have heard, he is always watching you."

"It was not an easy process," I admitted. "Which is what took so long. It would not have been possible without this woman's help. I'm afraid we both need to seek shelter at the People's Base. She has intimated that your shop has a tunnel leading there."

"Yes. Yes. Bonnie is a real help. It's a blessing you found her," she said. "Please, follow me." Anna led us through a door that opened to a stairway. As we got higher, the sound of a child's laughter rang high and clear. It was a sound I hadn't heard in a few days: real laughter. For a moment, I envied the child, able to experience such joy despite her circumstances.

She had lost everything, too. Her parents and home were history and she was being raised by neighbors. I hoped Frank had followed through and sent them money, but I somehow knew that even if he had not, these people would provide for Rose, no matter the cost.

When we reached the top of the stairs, Anna called out, "Hank! Hank! Come out here now!"

Male grunting trailed behind Anna's command. A man met us in the doorway leading to the kitchen and his eyes widened in disbelief. "Blossoms and Roots!" He exclaimed and hurried himself into a bow. Anna, realizing she hadn't curtseyed, squeaked and rushed into one.

"What's going on?" An approaching child's voice said. When Rose appeared, she didn't curtsey; she ran over and wrapped her arms around me. "Oh! Queen Miriam! I am so happy to see you!"

Hank and Anna looked on, slightly horrified at the girl's lack of propriety. I nodded and smiled at them, to reassure them that it was alright. Being raised in Evergreen Palace, I was always expected to be proper; something I frequently forgot as a little girl. I hardly expected any child to be held to the same expectations adults were. That being said, I hardly expect adults to always remember those standards either.

"I am happy to see you, too, Rose," I responded to the little one, returning her hug without bending over.

"Hank, Queen Miriam needs our help," Anna whispered loudly to the man I was assuming was her husband.

Hank's eyebrows rose to his forehead. "Anything for you, my Queen of Hearts," he said with a knowing look. I sighed with relief when I heard the name the rebels called me. I didn't know what happened to turn my luck, but I was grateful for the change.

"Thank goodness. I need –" I tried to come up with a way to ask about the People's Base without saying it outright. I knew he was involved, but I didn't know if Anna was. By the way he was looking at me, I was thinking she didn't know. "I need to find someone who can help me contact the rebels."

"Oh! Hank can do that!" Little, oblivious Rose proclaimed. "He knows lots of people!"

"Come along, Rose. Let's let the Queen and Hank chat," Anna said, taking the child by the hand and removing her from the room. Rose waved at me widely on the way out, and I waved back.

"She is sweet. Thank you for taking care of her," I said to Hank.

"She is a darling girl. Her parents were good people." Hank looked wistfully after Anna and Rose, and I wondered how familiar with Rose's family they were. "So," he began, returning to the topic at hand. "We were told to keep an eye out for you. Come with me. There is actually an entrance to the People's Base right beneath my store."

Truly, my good fortune was astounding me. Any moment, I felt like the world was going to crumble apart at my feet again. But nothing like that happened.

Hank reopened the door to the stairway, and Bonnie and I followed him down the stairs, back into storage, through a different trapdoor than the one we came in, through some tunnels, to a secure trapdoor, to a secure porthole, into the Petrichorian People's Base.

The sight that greeted me was a long clear wall that separated the base from water, which I was assuming was the Petrichorian Sound. Fish and seals were swimming about and I couldn't help but be awed by the view.

As we followed Hank, I lost track of turns and became hopelessly lost. We walked for several minutes until, finally, Hank knocked on a door.

"A moment!" I heard shouted in a familiar Southlander drawl. I was sure my entire face lit up before he even opened the door.

Hank brought himself into another bow and Bonnie curtseyed when Harrison opened the door. They stayed that way for a few moments while Harrison stared at me, completely dumbfounded. I cleared my throat and moved my eyes in a gesture toward them, and Harrison finally realized he was forgetting another person was there.

"Roots! Sorry, man. Please stand." Harrison forcefully took Hank's hand in his and shook it enthusiastically. Before moving on to Bonnie and doing the same. "What's your name?"

I covered my mouth with my hand to hide a chuckle. Hank and Bonnie now looked as dumbfounded by Harrison's behavior as Harrison was to see me show up at his door.

That was definitely a huge difference between our cultures. Arborians were raised to treat Nobility and Royalty with deference. While the Nobility and Royalty were well-respected in Southland, they were nowhere near as proper in speech or etiquette as Arborians.

"Uh," Hank eyeballed me and I nodded, encouraging him to go with it. "Hank, Your Highness. This is Bonnie. She brought Queen Miriam to my shop so we could bring her here."

"Well, Hank, Bonnie, come right on in." Harrison pulled him in. Upon releasing Bonnie's hand, he picked me up and swirled me around into the room. I squealed like a twenty-first century teenage girl at a boy band concert and he laughed. "Rose, how the heck did you get here so quickly? I was just about to round everyone up to make a plan to spring you out of the pen."

Smiling, I shrugged and said, "Well, when I woke up, Frank was just returning to the room. He was drunk and tired." Remembering that we were not alone, I decided to temporarily leave out the part about using my ability on Frank and the vision I had had before Lucas got me out of the love stupor Duke Sandran put me in.

"I was able to convince him that Duke Sandran's ability was still at work. After I suggested that we cancel Court for the morning,

I said I should walk around town alone so the people could see I was no longer a prisoner, but with Frank of my own will. He agreed it was a great idea, said to bring guards with me, and proceeded to go to bed.

"The guards didn't want to go into Bonnie's lingerie shop, so they confidently set guards up at the external entrances, not knowing she had another beneath the shop that led to Hank's grocer. I must have had angels working extra hard to get me here because it has just been one good thing after another today."

Finally able to get a breath in, I plopped down on a sofa in his sitting area.

"If Princesses do not plop, Queens certainly do not, my Queen of Hearts," a familiar voice said, coming out from the bathroom.

I jumped up and threw myself at my tutor. "Doctor Bartholomew! I have been so worried about you! What are you doing here?"

Doctor Bartholomew patted my back awkwardly and Harrison laughed behind me. "I have *been* here the whole time, Queen Miriam. Prince Harrison and I were discussing plans to help you escape the palace, but it appears you have figured it out on your own."

"She's a smart woman, Doc," Harrison said.

Doctor Bartholomew bristled at his informality, but didn't correct him. Harrison was a Prince, after all. Harrison turned to Hank. "Hank, Bonnie I request that you bring your family down here until this whole thing blows over for your safety. Someone may have seen Queen Miriam enter your shop, but not leave. Hank if you want to bring down whatever perishables your grocer has, so they don't spoil before you can sell them, we'll pay for them and use them in the kitchen."

Harrison walked over to his desk and jotted a note on a piece of stationary. "Bring this to level three and you'll get some assistance bringing your family and belongings down here."

Hank took the note and shook his head, with astonishment, not disobedience. "Thank you, Your Highness. You are most kind." He met my eyes. "I look forward to the true beginning of your reign, my Queen of Hearts. If you require anything from my family again, please let me know."

"Of course, Hank. Thank you very much for everything. And thank you again, Bonnie."

With the dismissal, Hank and Bonnie left the room. I walked back to the couch, but before I could plop, Doctor Bartholomew cleared his throat. Sighing, I lowered myself slowly onto the seat. Some things never change.

Chapter 28

A while later, the Princes, Generals, Doctor Bartholomew, and I stood around a blueprint of Evergreen Palace. Much to my chagrin, I needed to give away the locations of a few of the secret entrances for the invasion. There were still a few Frank didn't know about. I not only had to give them away for Evergreen Palace, but for each of the Nobility's grand houses. It was something Father made me memorize for when I was visiting other provinces.

As I was being seduced and reduced to becoming Frank's doll, Prince Liam and the Atlanteans were bringing the combined armies up to the Petrichorian People's Base via submarine. I wondered about the size of the vessels and how many trips it took to get everyone up there, but didn't ask about it. It didn't seem pertinent to the plan.

Really, it was fairly simple. Synchronously, we would attack Evergreen Palace at the same time the People's Bases all over Arboria invaded the Noble houses. Frank had set up his military in each province to surround each Noble house, just as he set the military up around Evergreen Palace. Sequoia's people were stationed just outside the New California border, awaiting their orders.

The tunnels we would be using all opened out beyond the military perimeters, and were well-hidden. To avoid being seen, we would be filtering our armies into the tunnels in small groups. Once everyone was situated, we would invade and retake each house and the palace.

Orders were to kill only if necessary. Given that I had personal experience with more than one siren, I knew that it was very possible that not everyone in Frank's military was there actually by choice. We would capture and imprison everyone we could, then Harrison, Lucas' band, and other mind-readers would do a tour of the provinces. Starting in Petrichoria, Lucas would sing to the prisoners a version of the song he sung to me to break Duke Sandran's hold. From there, Harrison and the other mind-readers would interview the prisoners to determine if they were really volunteers. There were only four other mind-readers in Arboria that we knew of, though, so it would still be a long process.

I shared my vision of Harrison and Frank in battle. All but Harrison were surprised to find out I even had visions. From what I gathered, it was unusual for someone like us to have more than one gift. I had three. Was I a freak or something?

Harrison squeezed my hand and assured me that if it came down to a battle between Frank and him, he would come out on top. The rest of the men agreed and I felt irritated that no one was taking me seriously.

I reiterated the importance that everyone listen. I explained my past visions that had come to pass. But everyone agreed that regardless of the vision, now was the time to attack. While I hated it, I had to agree.

When Frank figured out that I had escaped, and wasn't out for a day on the town, he would be vulnerable. He had banished everyone left at Evergreen Palace that I cared about, so he had nothing to hold over me anymore. Our strongest forces were there in Petrichoria, where Frank's greatest fortification was.

It really was the best time, even if it did put Harrison's life in danger. When we were finished discussing plans, we prayed that God would lead us against our enemy, then adjourned.

I was staring at my tapping fingers when Prince Leonardo approached me. "Queen Miriam, may I speak with you?"

"Of course, Prince Leonardo." He raised an eyebrow. "Leon," I corrected myself and Leon smiled. "Harrison, could you give us a moment?" Harrison nodded with understanding and left us alone. We sat down next to each other.

Leon gently placed his hand on mine. "Miriam, I wanted – no – I needed you to know something. About what happened to Domonique, I do not blame you." My lower lip quivered and I bit it. "Truly, it is not your fault. It was Frank and Prince Phineas, who is already being extradited back to Britainnia to face trial for his crimes. He will pay, Miriam, for what he did to us. I will ensure it. As soon as I assist in placing your kingdom back into your loving hands, I will head straight there to make sure those he was responsible for killing are represented."

I nodded, unable to speak, and squeezed his hand in mine. Our eyes met, and I saw in him a real friend. He understood, at least partially, what I was going through. While he still had family at home, he did lose a sister. He knew what it felt like to lose someone you love.

"For what it is worth, you are the bravest woman I have ever known," Leon continued. "For you to still move forward despite all you have been through, I cannot begin to know how you do it. You are an inspiration." Leon stood, kissed my hand, and left me in the map room.

I resumed tapping my fingers, thinking of the many ways everything could go wrong. Frank could have found the tunnels I talked about in our meeting. They could be guarded if he did. Harrison could die. *I* could die. Prince Liam and Prince Leonardo could die, causing a fracture between our kingdoms. Frank's people could refuse surrender and even more people could die. Death, death, and death! My head felt like it was going to explode.

As macabre thoughts raced through my mind, Harrison and Doctor Bartholomew re-entered the room. Doctor Bartholomew placed a document in front of me and smiled. That was weird.

Taking the document in my hand, I looked it over. It was a Queen's Decree divorcing myself from Frank. I quickly shot Doctor Bartholomew a look. "Is this for real?"

"Indeed. It is signed by the Delegates and newly appointed Representatives from each province. The only thing it is missing is your signature."

"Representatives?"

"After much discussion, the Delegates and King's test participants decided all positions of power in the government, aside from the Royalty, should be elected. The Representatives will take over the roles the Nobility now plays. The King's Test participants were appointed by the Delegates to be the first Representatives. In the future, they will be elected the same way Delegates are."

I let that sink in, a little miffed at not being involved with the decision, but having no issue with it. I asked, "And this will divorce Frank and me?"

"Indeed."

I looked at Harrison. "If I sign this now, I want you to marry me before we begin funneling people out for the attack." Harrison smiled big.

"Why do you think I am here, my Queen?" Doctor Bartholomew asked me like I was an idiot. "I am an ordained minister after all."

"You are? Since when?"

"A few years ago. True that I do not have my own congregation, but I am ordained."

"And you will marry Harrison and me?"

Doctor Bartholomew let out an exasperated sigh. "Truly, Queen Miriam, you have a gift for the obvious."

Without further hesitation, I signed the document. Harrison pulled me to my feet, held both my hands in his, and we were married right there in the map room. He had rings in his pocket that we placed on each other's fingers. We would have a big wedding with pomp and circumstance another time. All that mattered was that we were able to stand united against Frank.

When we were finished, Doctor Bartholomew produced the Arborian King and Queen's crowns as if by magic. He placed them on our heads, and pronounced Harrison King of Arboria.

"Now," I said. "Let's go reclaim our kingdom."

Chapter 29

We were done. We were fed up. There was no need for a rallying speech because everyone was already on the same page. The Generals and Princes passed the plans down to their subordinates, who passed it down to theirs, who passed it on to theirs, and so on until each and every person knew what we were going to do.

The Princes, Generals, and I met at the exit and nodded to each other in solidarity. We all wore hooded cloaks over our military uniforms. Harrison had a uniform made for himself and, apparently, I already had one I didn't know about. The uniforms were dark green and brown, patterned in such a way to camouflage us against a dark Arborian night. Our hooded cloaks were black. We still wore our emerald and diamond studded crowns under our hoods.

Harrison led the first group out of the base and into the tunnel. It took us the whole night and next day to get everyone out and stationed in the tunnels. I stood at the door and prayed over each group that left. When the second to last group made it, they commed us. It was time for the last group to leave. We prayed together, then headed out.

We exited through a different opening than the one I used when I came in through the grocer. The opening let out in the middle of the forest surrounding the back perimeter of Evergreen Palace. The ten of us crept quietly through the trees; in that part of the forest, there were no paths, so we had to be careful with our feet, and keep our eyes on the lights emanating from the palace.

I couldn't help but wonder what Frank was thinking at the moment. He had to know by now that I was really gone. Would he punish Duke Sandran, thinking he lied about the effectiveness of his ability or would he assume that I had found another siren to get me back into my right mind?

My mind then strayed to Harrison and the vision. I didn't want to think about the danger he would be in, but I couldn't stop the thoughts from going through my mind. I had only seen an image. One moment of horror. What would happen if the scene progressed? Would Harrison kill Frank? Or would the battle end with Frank's imprisonment? Or would Frank kill Harrison? Or would Frank have *me* kill Harrison, after all?

We made it to the tunnel, the other rebels slapping us on the back in welcome. I didn't tarry there, but moved on through the army of men and women willing to put their lives on the line for Arboria. The variety of people amazed me; I still couldn't get over how quickly Southland, Atlantis, New California, and New America came to our aid. Isolation was definitely going to be a thing of the past after this battle.

After a couple of minutes, I made it to Harrison. His hood was no longer up, and his crown blinked in the dim lighting of the tunnel. When I got to him, I threw my hood back as well and jumped into his arms.

"I'm so glad you're safe, Rose," He murmured into my hair.

"Me? You are the one who has been here all last night and all day today!" I responded.

"Well, you're here now." Harrison released me and brought his wrist-comm up to his mouth. "The Queen of Hearts has reached the Entrance of Hearts. King of Hearts is ready as well. Everyone else ready?"

"Princes of Diamonds are ready at the Entrance of Diamonds," came Prince Liam's voice. I could imagine Leon's swift head nod.

"General of Clubs is ready at the Entrance of Clubs," came the voice of General Lee.

"General of Spades is ready at the Entrance of Spades," said General Cook.

"General of Jokers is ready at the Entrance of Jokers," said General Madden.

Harrison looked to me, probably sensing my dread. Taking a deep breath, I nodded and took his hand. Harrison raised his hand as a signal to the army. The sounds of light guns being unholstered and charged filled the tunnel.

"Go," Harrison said into the wrist-comm, then shouted to the army, "Arboria!"

With a roar spreading over the army, Harrison threw open the door and everyone spilled into the hallway of offices. Harrison and I strolled down the center of the shouting and fighting rebels, making our way to the Core.

A glance into the Throne Room confirmed Frank was not there. Some of the rebels ran into the room and shot up the thrones. It was a huge waste of weapon energy, but my heart lifted at the sight of chunks blowing off the seats and the Millerian flag being torn into strips of nothing.

I moved my gaze up the Core stairway and saw Frank looking over the edge, eyes wild with fright and surprise. I grinned at him and pulled Harrison to come up the stairs with me. Frank's eyes got even bigger and I saw him retreat to our room – scratch that – *my* room.

As we approached the third floor, I looked down and saw several wounded on both sides of the conflict. However, the fighting was quieting down and Millerian soldiers were being forced to their knees with their hands on their heads in surrender. I smiled, feeling even more confident than I already was.

When Harrison and I approached the door to the King and Queen's suite, the two soldiers at the door stood firm for a moment. Long, foreboding looks from Harrison and me, not to mention shouts of "Long live the Queen of Hearts" being shouted from beneath us, eventually drew them to their own surrender. They both dropped to their knees, and one pressed the button to open the door.

I entered the room first, with Harrison close behind me. Frank stood in the middle of the room with his Millerian King's crown planted firmly on his head and the Millerian Queen's crown held in his hands.

"Not to sound cliché, but it's over Frank," I said to him. "Your men and women all over Evergreen Palace and all the province Noble houses are defeated." I assumed. "Surrender now and I will allow you to live."

Frank scoffed. "To what end, Rose? To go to trial, be condemned guilty, *then* killed? No. Not to sound cliché, but it's not over until I say it's over."

Frank thrust out a hand and said, "Come." My feet moved on their own volition to him.

"Stop it, Frank!" Harrison shouted and began to move toward him.

"No. *You* stop, Harrison," Frank countered, and Harrison stopped in his tracks.

How could I forget about this? Frank threatened this. How do we fight this?

I looked back to make sure Harrison heard me. His face twisted in anguish, telling me he had no idea how to solve this. I turned back to find a grinning Frank only a couple steps away.

248

Frank took his outreached hand and removed the Arborian Queen's crown from my head, and placed the Millerian one in its place.

"Much better," Frank muttered. Tracing a finger down my cheek with one hand, he unholstered the light gun at his side with the other. "Recognize this, my love?" He held the light gun up so I could see it.

"Looks just like every other black gun I have ever seen," I said in a tone full of the bravado I was actually lacking.

Frank chuckled.

"I hate your stupid laugh," I sneered, feeling a bit of release to finally get that out there.

Frank backhanded me, and I heard Harrison grunt with effort to be released from Frank's hold.

"Rose, Rose, Rose. You just never know when to shut up."

"Nope."

Frank slapped me full-on with his palm that time. "Answer the rotting question."

"I already did, you idiot! I don't recognize the weed-rotting gun!" I shouted at him.

"Well," Frank said in an eerily calm voice. "You should. This is the same weapon my father used to kill your father and mother. Guess what it's going to be used for now."

"No," I whispered. Harrison yelled with his struggle in the background. "Frank, please. Surrender. Even if you have me kill Harrison, you will still lose."

Frank placed the light gun in my hand and turned me around so I was facing Harrison. "Please," I begged in a shaky voice. Harrison stood stone still.

Caressing my shoulders, Frank said, "I'll tell you what, Rose. *You* surrender to *me* and I will let him live."

"I can't do that, Frank. I won't surrender my kingdom to you again." My hands raised, aiming the light gun at Harrison of Frank's accord.

"You misunderstand me, Rose," Frank said into my ear, then nibbled it. "Come with me into exile and he will live. And you won't have to live with the guilt of killing him."

Tears ran furiously down my cheeks and my head felt like it was splitting from the mental battle. "Harrison. Help."

"*Harrison. Help,*" Frank mocked and chuckled.

Suddenly, I felt Harrison's presence in my mind, and I was no longer fighting Frank on my own. Together, we pushed against his will. I could feel the liquid from my eyes thicken, and something was dripping from my ears. Blood. I knew because Harrison looked the same.

I shifted a foot, then the other so I was facing Frank. He held out his hands to mollify me. "Now Rose, remember the last time you fought me."

I struggled to speak. "Now Frank – the gun – is pointing – at you. Release us – immediately – or else." I charged the gun.

Frank slowly lowered himself to his knees, placed his hands on his head, and screamed. Feeling more confident than ever, I pushed a little further at him, mentally showing him how much I loathed him, how I would always think of him as a monster, and he would lose his power when I was done with him. I felt a few drops of blood drip from ear canal and hit my neck.

We continued to struggle until I felt a release and the room went quiet, except for the sound of Harrison falling behind me and panting. The light gun held firmly with my right hand, I wiped my eyes, cheeks, and neck with the other, and sighed in relief.

Frank lay unmoving on the ground and I wondered if he was dead. Cautiously, I went over and tapped him with my foot. He still didn't move. Bending over, I felt for a pulse. He had one, but it was faint and he showed no signs of waking any time soon.

"Rose, is it over?" Harrison breathed.

"Yes. It is," I said thickly.

Chapter 30

Shortly after Frank's collapse, Harrison was able to pull himself up and shout down for help. Leon was the one to come into the room with a set of magnacuffs. Of course, before cuffing him, Leon punched Frank squarely in the jaw, even though he was unconscious. If it were anyone else, I might have cared. Since Frank was directly responsible for the death of Leon's sister, I thought Leon was rather merciful.

Leon tossed Frank over his shoulder and we marched down the stairs. Stopping at the railing of the second floor to show a captured Frank off to our people, we smiled and nodded at the applause bursting from the Core of Evergreen Palace. Arborians, Southlanders, Atlanteans, Californians, and Americans shouted and screamed in victory. Prince Liam, General Madden, General Lee, and General Cook joined us on the second story.

"All other attacks have gone as well as this one, Queen Miriam," Prince Liam yelled to me over the din. "The kingdom of Arboria is yours once again."

Tears in my eyes, I gripped the hands of my allies and spoke words of gratitude to each one. Turning back to my people, I held my hands out to quiet the crowd.

"Arborians!" I shouted, and the crowd erupted into cheers again. I allowed the victorious shout to last a long moment, then quieted them again.

"Arborians and allies, though time may tell us it hasn't been very long, we know that it has been an arduous fight to retake this great kingdom from a foul force.

"We have lost loved ones," I choked on the words, then cleared my throat. "But their loss was not in vain. I am honored to be your Queen, but I would not be standing here today if it were not for you all. Arboria is as much yours as it is mine." I took Harrison's hand in mine and held it up. "Ours. Last night, Prince Harrison of Southland became my husband and King Harrison of Arboria." Frank shot a look of shock at me.

A random shout of "Long Live the Queen and King of Hearts" came up from the corner, beginning a domino effect until everyone in the palace was chanting it. I had to silence the crowd again to continue the speech.

"For those of you who fought on the side of the traitor, Francis Miller, this is not the end for you. I know from personal experience the power not only he has, but one in his employ has. There will be an investigation into each of your cases to determine your innocence or guilt. It may take some time, but I promise you true justice rather than blind vengeance.

"This is a time that will be remembered by all of us. We will tell this story to our children, and they will tell theirs until it becomes history. Just as the story of the first King Alexander and his journey is history to us today.

"Today will be a day we hold dear from now on. It is not only the end of a year, but the beginning of a new age in Arboria. I declare this day, The Day of Reminding. Each year, we will remind ourselves and future generations of our victory against treachery and the lives that victory cost us.

"Once these prisoners are transferred to the Petrichorian Prison, those of you who have not been assigned there will be dismissed for the day. It will take time to rebuild and I pray for your patience and willingness to help when called upon.

"Thank you all! Good night!" Cheers and applause filled the air again, and I saw prisoners being ushered out of the palace. A rebel approached Leon and offered to take Frank to the prison, an offer Leon refused. I couldn't blame him. If I wasn't so sick of seeing his face, I would have wanted to see him tightly locked in a cell. As it was, I would take Leon's word for it.

The next several months went according to plan. After the investigation led by Harrison and Lucas, we found out many of Frank's soldiers had, indeed, been swayed with Duke Sandran's ability. When they awakened from their long mental slumber, they were horrified at the atrocities that took place at their hands. Most offered military service to atone for their misdeeds, though I certainly didn't ask it, or expect it, of them.

When Frank awoke, it was discovered that he had a stroke, similar to the one I had when I mentally fought him off, that rendered his body useless from the waist down. Because I was feeling vindictive, I didn't allow the surgery to provide him use of his legs again. He was tried and found guilty of treason, just as everyone suspected he would be.

While many, including Harrison, wanted his blood, I felt it was too easy an escape for him. I decided Frank should live life in prison, always separated by a wall from any person. Not only would that prevent him from being able to use his gift, but it would also give him the added consequence of isolation. Between that and forever being paralyzed because of the abuse of his abilities, I felt he was properly disciplined.

Prince Leonardo informed me that Britainnia did not make the same decision for Prince Phineas. He was tried and found guilty of treason against their Crown, and aiding in the assassination of their King and Queen along with a foreign King and Queen, my parents. He was hung. I didn't even know anyone did that anymore.

By August of that summer, Arboria was well on its way to being rebuilt. Harrison and I gave the people the wedding we promised ourselves and our people. Parties were held all over Arboria and Southland in celebration of the historic uniting of our kingdoms.

While I didn't know for sure that my parents and other loved ones were looking down upon me with smiles on their faces, I imagined it often enough. I may have lost all of them, but I still had Harrison and I knew that together, we would make a new life, a new family to belong to.

For a time, I had forgotten everything that was real and true about my life. When I needed it most, I remembered everything about it. Though my true life was nearly stolen from me by evil men, new friends reminded me of what was real. I knew what my life was then, but it wasn't over. Not at all.

Epilogue

"Harrison!" I shouted from our bed. Doctor Quincy stood next to me, checking my vitals. Again. I slapped away his hands. "You just did that, Doctor Quincy. Knock it off. HARRISON!" I shouted his name louder this time.

Doctor Quincy sighed, but spoke in a tone that belied his exasperation with me. "My Queen of Hearts, you know King Harrison is not home yet. He is on his way back from Representative Robert's estate in Maple."

"I don't care if he was visiting his sister in Southland! Whose bright idea was it, anyway, for him to go to Maple at a time like this?"

"Yours, my Queen of Hearts." Doctor Quincy smiled at me and I shot him a dirty look, which only made him chuckle at me.

"You think this is funny?"

"Oh. Absolutely, my Queen of Hearts." He tried for my pulse. Again.

I slapped his hands away. Again.

Just then, Harrison finally showed up. "Well, it's about time, *dear*." I managed to say "dear" like a curse word and Doctor Quincy chuckled again.

"I came as fast as I could, darlin'," Harrison drawled. I could tell he was nervous because his accent was thick. "Ya know I woulda been here faster if I coulda."

"Ugh. Relax. I hate when you combine words that shouldn't be combined."

Harrison looked at Doctor Quincy with a brow raised as if asking a question.

Doctor Quincy understood. "This is all perfectly normal, my King of Hearts."

"Stop talking about me like I'm not here!" I shouted at both of them. "How much longer?" I whined. "I don't want to do this anymore. I'm done. Can I be done now? I'm done."

Harrison chuckled. "Don't laugh at me!" I yelled with tear-filled eyes.

"Aw, honey. I'm not laughing at you. I love you," Harrison said as he sat next to me and took my hand, which I squeezed super hard. He tried, unsuccessfully, not to flinch.

"Ahhhh! I think it's time!" I shouted.

"Very well," Doctor Quincy said with infuriating serenity while he checked. "Oh, yes. Definitely. I can see his head. Give him a push, Your Majesty."

I did. "This. Is. Painful!" I breathede after the push and looked at Harrison. "This is harder than I remember."

"Well, that *was* a false life, Rose," Harrison saide.

"Shut up!" I shouted through another push, irritated by his logic at a time like this.

Harrison breathed with me and held his breath when I pushed, which was driving me a little nuts, but I was too busy to shout at him about it, or anything else, anymore. After twenty long minutes of pushing, our little Prince was born. The relieving sound of a baby's cry resounded, and Harrison and I smiled at each other.

Doctor Quincy cleaned up our baby boy and placed him gently in my arms. It took him no time at all to find my breast and latch on, the blond tuft of hair on his head tickling me as he ate. "Aw. My little baby," I said, then began to cry.

I thought about my little Thomas and Harmony, knowing that unless I brought them up in my dreamscape, I wouldn't see them again. But this little one, he wa s real. And he was mine.

Doctor Quincy brought out the birth certificate and asked for the new Prince of Arboria's name. "Stephan," Harrison and I said in unison. We had agreed on the name long ago. Stephan was the first of my loved ones that I lost and we found it appropriate that my new loved one be named for him.

Doctor Quincy jotted the name and all other information down, promised to send us an official copy, and took his leave.

Harrison tickled Stephan's busy chin with a couple fingers. "Little Prince Stephan, welcome to a free and wonderful world. Your family loves you and your people will, too."

Acknowledgements

First, and foremost, I would like to thank God for everything He has done for me. Most specifically, I thank Him for His inspiration and gift of writing.

I would not have been able to the Rose of Petrichoria series, without the support of my family at The Barn. Thank you for all your encouragement and love! My husband, Nick, was gracious enough to let me use his idea of the Daze for the pandemic in this series.

Several people read through and critiqued Reminded and I am appreciative for all of you, too: Lynnette Bonner, Sheri Mast, Becky Luna, Deborah Wyatt, Cara Koch, Rachel Custer, Mary Griffith, and Vanessa Thalhofer.

Note From The Author

Forgetting your life, or knowing someone who has, is a horrible experience. In 2007, my mother suffered strokes while recovering from quadruple bypass heart surgery. One of the debilitating consequences was a loss of short-term memory. Over time, her vascular dementia progressed to the point that she most often didn't remember most long-term memories either. On November 27, 2017, my mother, Judith LeFebvre Gosvener, was brought out of her illness here on Earth to blessed wholeness in Heaven

If you have a loved one who is living with dementia, it is understandable that it would be difficult to see them go through it, or even to experience the heartbreak when they don't recognize you. People with dementia don't have the luxury of remembering your last visit. They live in the here and now. While it may be hard for you to see them, give them the love and respect they continue to deserve because they are still human beings with human feelings.

They have forgotten, do not forget them.

About The Author

Katie Hauenstein was educated at Northwest University in Kirkland, Washington, where she met and married her husband, Nick Hauenstein. After graduating with her Bachelor's Degree in Communication, she had her daughter, Mary, and began writing her stories. Forgotten, the first book in the Rose of Petrichoria series, is her first published novel.

In her spare time, you can find Katie binge watching superhero/sci-fi/fantasy shows on Netflix, fangirling about Doctor Who, attending a variety of movies at the local theater, or with her nose in a book. She also enjoys cake decorating, online shopping, and other introverted activities.

Made in the USA
Columbia, SC
20 April 2018